MONSTER BOGEY

Bogeys, snot, gloop, boogers . . . what do you call the stuff up your nose? Whatever you call it, could you make a monster out of it? Well, Frank does. And when lightning strikes, he gets a lot more than he bargained for when it comes to life. It's a sticky situation, but Bogey monster might just be the answer to defeating the true evil facing Frank and his friends. Full of gross-out laughter, loyalty and adventure, this debut is a top pick by brand-new talent, Anna Brooke.

BARRY CUNNINGHAM
Publisher
Chicken House

MONSTER BOGEY

ANNA BROOKE Illustrated by OWEN LINDSAY,

Chicken House

2 Palmer Street, Frome,
Somerset BA11 1DS

Text © Anna Brooke 2023
Illustrations © Owen Lindsay 2023

First published in Great Britain in 2023
Chicken House
2 Palmer Street
Frome, Somerset BA11 1DS
United Kingdom
www.chickenhousebooks.com

Chicken House/Scholastic Ireland, 89E Lagan Road, Dublin Industrial Estate,
Glasnevin, Dublin D11 HP5F, Republic of Ireland

Anna Brooke has asserted her right under the Copyright, Designs and Patents Act
1988 to be identified as the author of this work.

This book is a work of fiction. Names, characters, businesses, organizations, places,
events and incidents are either the product of the author's imagination or used in a
fictitious manner. Any resemblance to actual persons, living or dead, events or locales
is purely coincidental.

Designed and typeset by Steve Wells
Printed and bound in Great Britain by CPI Group (UK) Ltd, Croydon CR0 4YY

FSC
www.fsc.org
MIX
Paper | Supporting
responsible forestry
FSC® C171272

3 5 7 9 10 8 6 4 2

British Library Cataloguing in Publication data available.

PB ISBN 978-1-913696-58-0
eISBN 978-1-913696-81-8

For Maximillian,
my own little miracle of life!

BOOK
WARNING

Dear _____
  (insert your name here),

  Don't tell grown-ups about this book.
They'll think it's so ghastly, they'll
be sick in their socks. For inside is a
terrifying tale about revolting things like:
* bogey towers
* squelchy monsters
* slug goo
* slimy moats
and
* snot trails
  And at the end . . . well, at the end,
there's an enormous . . . Hang on! I'm
not telling you about the end. You can
start at Chapter 1 just like everyone
else.
  Honestly!

Frank

CHAPTER 1

A LITTLE MAN!

Have you ever picked your nose?

Don't lie, now.

I bet you have. I haven't, of course. I would never do anything revolting like that.

But I bet *you* have. And that's OK, because if you have, you can be friends with Frank.

Here he is, a skinny, freckly boy with curly red hair and his finger always up his nozzle.

His full name is **Frank Bear Horace Pickerty-Boop**, but for the sake of this story, we'll just call him Frank.

Frank had grown up in Snozzle Castle on the edge of Honkerty Village. Snozzle Castle was an old spooky-looking building with:

* **overgrown gardens**
* **a rickety bell tower**
* **a holey roof**
* **a forbidden dungeon**
* **a gloopy green moat**

and

* **cross-eyed gargoyles with dribbling chops**

It sounds grand, but it wasn't.

Frank's dad, a horror film maker, had received it as a gift from his 'biggest fan', but he and Mum, an opera singer, couldn't afford the repairs, so the family lived in the West Wing – in two tiny bedrooms, a teensy lounge with a teeny kitchen, and a tiddly bathroom with a toilet that did a little burp when it flushed. **Buurpp!** The East Wing lay abandoned except for old furniture, dangerous potholes, dusty paintings, bats and spiders that sang cabaret. And it was (like the dungeon) strictly OFF LIMITS to Frank.

Inside Snozzle Castle

So, as I was saying, Frank was a nose-picker, though he never ate his bogeys (for that would be really disgusting). Instead, he rolled them into little balls and saved them in his pocket until he got home from school. Then, when no one was looking, he emptied them into the wood-panelled cupboard in his bedroom.

Not even his mum or dad knew about the cupboard. They HATED bogeys (like all parents do) and were always telling him to 'stop picking'. Frank was sure they'd stop loving him if they found out. But he couldn't stop himself. He was proud of his heap, and over time, he'd piled so many boogers, he had a big bogey tower ...

75 centimetres ...

81 centimetres ...

97 centimetres ...

Frank was aiming for a metre.

Tiffany is Frank's best friend. She has curly brown ringlets and stick-outy ears. She lives on the other side of the village, with her mum, dad and 102-year-old great-gran.

Frank and Tiffany did everything together. Tiffany was the only other person in the entire world to know about the tower and the cupboard. But she didn't collect bogeys. She loved animals and collected slugs, and dreamt about one day setting up her own slug circus act. She carried four pet ones around with her in a jar: Sammy, Violet, Peach and Slim.

Every day after school, or in the holidays like now, the friends would play together in Frank's bedroom until teatime, setting agility courses for the slugs and collecting lovely trails of slug goo, which was perfect for holding the bogey tower together. It was funny, but the bigger the tower, the more it looked like a little man . . .

Now, on the evening this story begins, there was a . . . Oh, hang on. Have you got your wellies on?

No? Well, go and get them. And grab an umbrella too, because on the evening this story begins, there was a thunderstorm. And not just any thunderstorm. A thunderstorm so huge that the wind howled down the chimneypots like a ghost train whistle and the thunder rumbled so loudly that Frank's sweet old neighbour, Mrs Sniff, mistook the growl for her own little burp and said, 'Pardon me.'

And the rain. Oh, the rain. How it hammered, how it poured. Even the drooling gargoyles on Snozzle Castle had to take shelter inside the bell tower, and Lucy Longlegs, the star of the spiders' cabaret, sang 'Singin' in the Rain' from underneath a bucket in the East Wing.

But worst of all, the rainwater battered extra holes into Snozzle Castle's roof, and droplets started to fall through the rafters and the cobwebs into Frank's bogey cupboard.

CHAPTER 2

BOO-A-WOO!

'QUICK!' Frank screamed, as he rushed over to drag his precious tower away from the drips. Water was bad for bogeys.

Tiffany joined him and together they heave-hoed the tower to the middle of the threadbare carpet and safety. Frank took a closer look, checking every inch for water damage. Where the drops had landed, little mounds had risen.

He frowned. 'The top's all squelchy.'

'It's all wavy, like a curly hairdo,' said Tiffany. 'What are you going to do?'

'Use this, for a start.' Frank pulled a hairdryer out from under a pile of clothes and started blow-drying the wet bits. Then, when he was satisfied that the rain had done no lasting harm, he breathed a sigh of relief and said, 'Now I need to hide it somewhere dry.'

But WHERE?

The tower was too tall to hide under his bed, too wide to fit into his wardrobe and too heavy to lift into his wash basket. And he couldn't leave it in the middle of the room or Mum and Dad would find it in five seconds flat.

Suddenly, thunder ROARED outside, the lights flickered on and off, and Mum's singy-songy voice floated down the corridor.

'CHILDREEEEN!'

Frank and Tiffany jumped.

They could hear her footsteps in the hallway.

'We've got to find somewhere to hide it. NOW!' Frank said.

'But where? But where?' cried Tiffany.

'I don't know, I don't know.' Frank jumped up and down

on the spot (jumping helped him think).

Then, what happened next happened quickly:

WHOOSH!

Did you get that?

No?

Here it is again.

WHOOSH!

Still too fast? OK, I'll slow it down.

Frank spotted his unmade bed and whipped off the sheet. Next, he told Tiffany to rush over and close the secret bogey cupboard. As Mum knocked on the bedroom door, Frank threw the sheet over the tower and felt his heart do a little somersault, leap into his mouth and bounce on his tongue – **BOING BOING BOING**.

'Boo-a-woo,' he spluttered, which isn't a word at all.

'Ah, playing ghosts, are you?' Mum smiled as she came into the room, looking at the sheet and mistaking the 'boo-a-woo' for a spooky 'WOOOOOOOO'.

Frank and Tiffany nodded. They couldn't believe their luck.

'WOOOOOOOO,' added Frank, just to make sure.

'Well, can you tear yourselves away? *Raindrops keep falling on my head,*' she sang operatically, before putting on her *I'm worried about what next door will say* face. 'The roof must have new holes – water's coming through the kitchen ceiling – so I need you to help me and Dad put some saucepans under the drips.'

Frank nodded again, his heart slowing to a normal rhythm. Mum and Dad were always worrying about their new neighbour, Willamina Honk. She'd only moved into the posh house next door, Snozzle Lodge, a year ago, but she kept posting nasty complaints about the scruffy state of the castle – like 'your garden's a dump!' and 'your moat stinks to high heaven!' – and it was REALLY getting to them.

'Come on, then, or we'll have a *flood in the oveeeeeen,*' Mum sang again, trying to sound chirpy.

And at that, Frank and Tiffany had no choice but to step out of the bedroom and follow Mum down the dimly lit hallway. Frank glanced back at his tower one last time, then carefully closed the door.

'Don't worry, it's hidden for *now*,' Tiffany whispered.

'Yeah, but we'll have to find somewhere better to hide it while the bogey cupboard dries,' Frank whispered back.

'I'll help you.' Tiffany winked. 'And the slugs will keep an eye on it while we're gone.'

And for a moment, Frank felt calm. Of course things would be OK. As soon as the storm was over, he and Tiffany would wipe the cupboard down, give it a quick blast with the hairdryer and have his tower back inside before you could say, *Just pick it, YEAH!*

But alas, dear nose-pickers . . . I mean readers . . . No, I mean nose-pickers . . . Frank couldn't have been more wrong, for something terrifying was about to happen, and life in Snozzle Castle would **NEVER, EVER, EVER** be normal again.

EVER.

CHAPTER 3

FRAZZLE, SIZZLE, CRACK

Are you scared yet? You should be. I told you something terrifying was about to happen and it's here in this chapter that it does. If I were you, I'd have an extra pair of pants on standby, because as Frank, Tiffany, Mum and Dad were placing saucepans under the drips in the kitchen, the storm took a turn for the worse. The grey, five o'clock sky turned as black as night and thick, eerie clouds swirled overhead with lightning forking out like flaming veins, striking the ground with ear-piercing crackles.

There was weirdness in the air. And not just over Snozzle Castle. All across Honkerty Village, the storm was making strange things happen.

Old Mrs Sniff saw the wind propel Clawdia, her Siamese cat, past the window.

Bo Jacobs the street performer watched his dancing hamster, Squishy, whoosh up a tree, bounce off a magpie and fall into a squirrel's nest (don't worry, she was still in her cage).

Walter Wills the grocer gawped as his blond toupee flew off and touched down between the poufy ears of one of Mrs Wirrel's giant grey poodles.

Gary Plonk the farmer stood aghast as his tractor set off on its own, zoomed up a ramp and landed perfectly in some bales of hay!

And Willamina Honk was whacked on the nose by a bag of sprouts that flew out of her fireplace.

ZOOM!

OUF!

'ARGH!'

Over at Snozzle Castle, the wind suddenly blew Frank's bedroom window open and the rain and leaves and some of Frank's dirty socks went whirling around the bogey tower.

When a second gust rushed in, it was the slugs' turn

for trouble, as Sammy, Violet, Peach and Slim found themselves sucked off their agility course into a tiny whirlwind that spiralled towards the bed at breakneck speed.

'MEEP!' squeaked Slim (which meant 'form a ring') as they spun like marbles. It was hard – a leaf had stuck to Peach's eye tentacles – but the brave gastropods managed to link up, head-to-tail, and freefall to the bed knob, where they landed like a hoop on a skittle.

At the same moment, the sheet covering the bogey tower shot up into the air and caught on the green balloon-shaped light fitting, where it billowed like a creepy flag, sending eerie shadows over the bogey tower's bobbly surface.

If you'd been in the room, you'd have sworn it looked like a stubby green goblin. It was a good job you weren't, because moments later, a fork of lightning hurtled through the window and struck the tower full on.

FRAZZLE
SIZZLE

CRACK

All went quiet for a second, then a strange gurgling noise sounded by the tower. No, hang on. It wasn't by the tower, it *was* the tower. And then, through the flickering darkness, two bright yellow eyes appeared, followed by two knobbly arms and two stumpy legs glistening with snot. And THEN, as the thunder shook the heavens outside – **CRASH, BANG, BOOM** – the bogey tower started to move.

One step . . .

There was the flash of an eye.

Two steps . . .

A chunky green finger jerked outwards.

Three steps . . .

The thing lurched forward with outstretched arms, crying, '**GOO-GOO-GOOEY!**'

IT WAS ALIVE!

CHAPTER 3½

JUST CHECKING IN

Are you OK, nose-pickers?

Did you have to change your pants?

No?

I did – just after the tower started snorting and then again when it said **goo-goo-gooey**.

But don't worry, all the creepy parts are over.

STOP! No. Sorry. They're NOT!

They're about to get MUCH WORSE. GRIM even.

If you want my advice, buy yourself a chocolate bar to nibble on during the scary bits. Don't get Tomlinson's

Extra Dark – I've heard it's made with mouse droppings.
But something nice from your local supermarket: Pippin's
Peanut Parcels are good, as are Rocko's Raspberry Swirls.
And if you like bananas, Bally-Wally Balls are absolute
scrumdiddles.

You have been warned.

Now, have you ever travelled back in time?

No?

Well, touch this black dot and see what happens.

Sorry, wrong one. Try this one instead.

CHAPTER 4

BROWN-GREEN JELLY

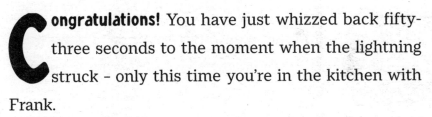

Congratulations! You have just whizzed back fifty-three seconds to the moment when the lightning struck – only this time you're in the kitchen with Frank.

'Whoa!' Frank cried, as the bang shook Snozzle Castle to its very core. Even the spiders in the rafters of the East Wing interrupted their cabaret routines to cling to their webs.

As the floor trembled in the kitchen, water sloshed out of the pans and formed puddles around the legs of the chairs and table. Dad was about to grab his phone to film the moody sky through the window, when he slipped on a wet patch and skidded towards the fridge like a human mop.

'EEK!'

CRASH!

'OUCH!'

Any other day, Frank would have giggled like a hyena. Today, he stared at Tiffany with worry in his eyes. There was a smell of trouble in the air (cherries mixed with hedgehog bum gas), and both friends could tell the bang had come from Frank's bedroom. Any second now, Mum and Dad – who, judging from their expressions, knew it too – would want to investigate.

'We've got to get there first,' Frank whispered to Tiffany. If they could buy themselves some time, even just a few seconds, they might just stop Mum and Dad from finding the tower.

Frank pulled open the kitchen door.

'Where are you two going? And why are you

whiiisperiiiiiinnnng?' Mum sang.

'My bedroom,' Frank replied guiltily, his index finger creeping up his nose, as it always did when he was nervous.

'Frank!' Mum cried in top C.

'Sorry!' POP! ('Twas the sound of his finger *popping* out of his nostril.)

Tiffany smiled innocently.

'Not on your own. That bang sounded dangerous. We're coming too,' said Dad, finally grabbing his phone and switching it to camera mode.

His words fell on deaf ears. Actually, they fell on NO ears (except Mum's), for Frank and Tiffany had already sprinted off down the hallway and were standing in front of the bedroom door.

As Frank pushed the door open, wind howled in through the open window, blowing leaves and socks into their faces.

COUGH, COUGH.

SPLUTTER, SPLUTTER.

For a second they couldn't see anything, then, as the wind settled and the debris fell to the floor, their jaws dropped.

There, by the open window, stood the bogey tower, only it wasn't a tower any more. It was a two-legged, two-armed THING, with a bobbly body and snot-rimmed toes. Its face was rugged with crinkles above its upturned nose. It was a . . . B-BOGEY MONSTER! And a MONSTER BOGEY!

Of course, *you* know that already, don't you? But Frank and Tiffany didn't, and they SCREAMED . . .

'AHHHHHHHHHHHHHHHHHHHHHHHHHHHHHHHHHHHHH!'

and . . .

'AHHHHHHHHHHHHHHHHHHHHHHHHHHHHHHHHHHHHHHHH!'

and . . .

'AHHHHHHHH, AHHHHHHHH, AHHHHHHHH!'

Then, when they could scream no longer, the monster let out a high-pitched gurgle of its own . . .

'GOO-GOO-GOOEY!'

Frank was seriously spooked, but a little voice in his head said *move towards it*. It wasn't Frank's own voice, it was an earwig, but Frank didn't know that and the earwig fell out straight after.

Unfortunately for him (Frank, I mean, not the earwig), it was a mistake. For as Frank stepped forward, the monster wobbled like brown-green jelly, as if it were afraid – and used its webbed hands and feet to shimmy up the radiator on to the window ledge.

'Stop,' Frank said. 'I won't hurt you.'

But the monster just blew a big, gloopy raspberry – **PFFFTTTTT!** Then, as another fork of lightning hissed through the skies, it leapt straight out of the window into the electric darkness!

**Bogey
monster**

CHAPTER 5

A QUICK QUIZ!

Nose-pickers, here's a quick quiz:

QUESTION NUMBER 1:

What would you do if you'd just discovered your bogey tower had become a monster?

☐ **A. Make fart noises with your armpit.**

☐ **B. Stuff your socks with mouldy garlic.**

☐ **C. DEFINITELY NOT tell your parents the truth.**

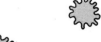

If you answered C, then you're just like Frank!

When Mum and Dad burst in asking 'Why all the screaming?', Frank didn't cry: **"CAUSE MY SECRET BOGEY TOWER'S NOW A MONSTER B-BOGEY THAT J-JUMPED OUT THE WINDOW!'** No. He just closed the window and pointed up at the sheet on the green balloon-shaped light fitting, and said they'd thought they'd seen a ghost. ('Twas a good lie – Mum had presumed they'd been playing ghosts earlier. Dad filmed it.)

QUESTION NUMBER 2:

When Tiffany's dad arrived straight after and it was time for her to scoop up the slugs and goooo (sorry, I meant to write 'go'), what do you think Frank said?

☐ **A. FLOBBER!**

☐ **B. Big bananas.**

☐ **C. Don't worry. I won't do anything 'til you come around tomorrow.**

Yeah, it's C again!

But then, as the friends waved goodbye on the front step and Frank squinted through the rain for any sign of the bogey monster, he knew he couldn't wait for tomorrow. He was going to have to look for it tonight, while Mum and Dad were asleep. Even if that meant doing it all on his own.

CHAPTER 6

A CLUSTER OF BOGEYS

'**N**ight,' shouted Frank as he wiggled into his pyjamas. He felt nervous, but he was doing everything as normal, so that Mum and Dad wouldn't suspect anything.

Climbing under his duvet, he picked his nose, and crossed his fingers that his parents would go to bed soon.

They didn't. Before they went to bed they decided to:

* ✳ **Attach plastic sheets to the kitchen ceiling to stop any more water getting through.**
* ✳ **Stress about Willamina Honk and her complaint**

letters.

* **Argue about how they were going to find the money to repair the roof.**

* **Make up with a quick snog (I know it's gross, but what Frank's parents lacked in money, they made up for in luuurve).**

* **Reminisce about their life in Paris in the BC era (Before Children), when Dad's scary films had won lots of awards and Mum had been an opera singer, before Dad's biggest fan had given him the castle.**

* **Have a quick sing-song for old times' sake, with Dad filming Mum hitting her operatic high notes.**

* **Put Dad's vintage DVD collection and movie figurines back on the now-dry shelves.**

And it took AGES.

Only when the grandfather clock in the hallway struck midnight did Frank finally hear Mum's snores rattle through the wall.

It was the sign he'd been waiting for.

He changed back into his daytime clothes, grabbed his coat and torch, then - with his heart beating like a big bass drum - set off towards the only place he knew the monster had gone: outside.

The rain had stopped, but it was well spooky: soupy grey clouds flitted past the pale moon, making the gargoyles shine like silver.

Somewhere in the distance, a wolf howled. It wasn't really a wolf. Just a strange hedgehog who enjoyed impersonating other animals (it did wolves and dolphins).

But Frank didn't know that, and his knees trembled so much that he slipped in some mud and slid towards . . . the moat!

'ARGH!'

That was close! Frank managed to stop himself and roll away from the edge. Dad said an eel with a three-foot mouth lived down there. He'd never been able to film it and no one else had seen it, but Frank didn't want to take any chances.

He wiped squelchy mud off his coat and torch. Then, suddenly, as the torch beam bobbed up and down over the ground, he saw something green and gloopy on a nearby rock.

Could it be . . .?

Nope. False alarm. It was moat slime.

But wait.

What was *that* next to it?

He felt strangely drawn to it, as if being pulled by a magnet. It gave him a tickly feeling inside his nose.

GOOLIEMALOOLIE!

It was a cluster of bogeys.

In the shape of a **HANDPRINT!**

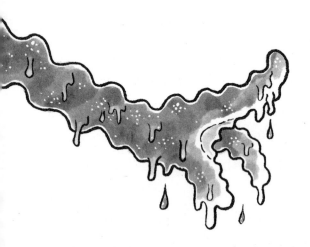

CHAPTER 7

DON'T HURT ME!

Frank's heart began to race. He shone the torch all around to look for more bogeys.

He found some. Over by Mum's favourite garden gnome and then again by the veggie patch. The monster had left a trail of snot - a recent one. The rain hadn't washed it away, so it had clearly been left AFTER the downpour!

He followed the bogey blobs all around the overgrown back garden - through the broken greenhouse, over the crumbly fountain, past the old orchard and the moat - to the abandoned East Wing. And then he saw it:

Another bogey handprint – only this time on a door.

Frank leapt for joy.

Then froze in fear.

Not because it was the door to the dangerous and spooky dungeon of the East Wing! Well, sort of that too. But because there, in a huddle by the door, was a **DARK, MONSTER-LIKE SHAPE!**

Chills ran down his spine and tap-danced on his bum.

He dropped his torch.

The thing moved towards him.

'AHHHHHHHHHHH!'

It pushed him over.

He fell on his back.

A bright light!

'DON'T HURT ME!' he blabbered.

'What are you doing here?' came a voice.

But it wasn't the bogey monster.

It was TIFFANY!

CHAPTER 8

A BIG BLACK HOLE!

The conversation that followed sounded like one of Dad's film scripts:

EXT. NIGHT. IN FRONT OF DANGEROUS AND SPOOKY DUNGEON DOOR

Eerie moonlight.

FRANK: What do you mean 'What am I doing here'? What are YOU doing here?

TIFFANY: I came to help, doh! I knew you'd look for the monster.

FRANK: How'd you get here?

TIFFANY: Bike.

FRANK: Woah! You're brave.

TIFFANY: Yep!

FRANK: Why'd you push me?

TIFFANY: I thought YOU were IT! You OK?

FRANK: Yeah.

TIFFANY: Why are you muddy?

FRANK: Fell over earlier.

TIFFANY: Want some salt-and-vinegar crisps?

FRANK: Yeah. Thanks.

CRUNCH CRUNCH CRUNCH CRUNCH

Frank was well pleased Tiffany was there. Hunting for the monster was seriously scary. Plus, she'd brought his favourite crisps and a head torch. And

Tiffany

the slugs were there in their jar, so if he thought about it hard enough and ignored his pounding chest, it was . . . well . . . the more the merrier!

'Look!' said Frank, pointing at the dangerous and spooky dungeon door. 'There's a bogey handprint here. I've been following a trail through the garden.'

'SOARING SLUGS!' said Tiffany. 'Maybe it's hiding in there?'

Now, if you ever have to choose between going into a forbidden dungeon to search for a scary monster and going home to scoff Jammie Dodgers in bed, choose the biscuits. You'll wake up with crumbs in your ears, but at least you won't have to fumble your way through a moat-slime-coated vault AND breathe fusty air filled with mushroom spores while worrying about being eaten alive.

Frank and Tiffany didn't have that choice. They didn't have any Jammie Dodgers. Plus, they were sure the monster was somewhere behind the door. They'd come this far. They couldn't turn back now.

Trembling in his muddy clothes like chocolate

blancmange, Frank gave the door a mighty push.

CREEEEEAAAAAK!

They stepped through and braced themselves for a monster meeting. Cobwebs and dust flew into their faces.

'This way,' spluttered Frank, his torch lighting up a dust-free spot.

They both rushed towards it, but … **BANG!** They tripped over a loose flagstone and went flying into a rusty old gate.

Their hands caught its bars, but the gate creaked forward and before they knew it, their feet had left the ground and they were swinging over a …

BIG BLACK HOLE!

CHAPTER 9

WE'RE GOING TO DIE!

'**A**HHHHHHHHHH!!!!!!!!!!' They kicked the air for something to stand on.

Frank's torch (which had been hanging on a cord around his wrist) fell off and plummeted into the gloom, smashing somewhere a LONG WAY DOWN.

'Did you see that?' squealed Tiffany.

'Yes,' cried Frank. **'WE'RE GOING TO DIE!'**

'No,' shouted Tiffany. 'There's a staircase by your left foot.' She turned her head torch towards it.

Frank stretched his leg, and (to his surprise) found that

she was right. Even though he was small, by extending his leg as far as it would go, he managed to get a full foot on a step.

'ONE, TWO, THREE.' He leapt off the gate to safety, then helped Tiffany do the same.

'**GOOLIEMALOOLIE**! That was close!' Frank gasped.

'**SOARING SLUGS** it was!' Tiffany gulped.

'**MEEP!**' agreed Sammy, Violet, Peach and Slim.

Panting with his back to the wall, Frank suddenly felt a tickle in his nose. He looked down to see that his hands were sticky.

'It's more of the monster's snot,' he said. 'Don't ask me why, but every time I've found some, my nose has felt weird. I think I've got a psychic connection with it – like we're bogey twins or something.'

'That adds up,' said Tiffany. 'It's made of your bogeys.'

'Well, it's definitely got as far as this gate,' said Frank.

'Do you think it went down there?' Tiffany asked, peering into the black.

'Bogeys come from dark, narrow nostrils, so it might

like dark, narrow hiding places,' Frank offered.

'It does look dark and narrow,' said Tiffany. 'Y-you sure you want to go?'

The air smelt like rotting moat slime, and Tiffany's head torch showed spiderwebs hanging like ghostly curtains, and crumbly walls glistening with damp, and – **GOOLIEMALOOLIE!** – was that a pile of bones?

'N-no.' Frank gulped. 'But if we want to find the monster, I think we have to go.'

And so off they went, like two trembling mice, **DOWN, DOWN** and **DOWN**.

CHAPTER 10

SNIFF... GROWL...GRUNT!

Now, if you've ever had to hunt for a bogey monster by walking down an uneven staircase to the bottom of a spooky dungeon you almost fell into, with nothing but a tiny head torch for light, you'll know how Frank and Tiffany were feeling.

What?

You've never done that before?

Well, let me tell you.

They were **PETRIFIED**. Pee-in-your-pants petrified.

And to make matters worse, the stairs descended into

a deep, dark chamber that turned every sound into an eerie **echo . . .** echo . . . echo. Then, once their feet had **crunched . . .** crunched . . . crunched . . . over Frank's broken **torch . . .** torch . . . torch, they found themselves inside a strange stone passageway that turned into an uphill tunnel with a low ceiling and a dirt floor.

'Why would a t-tunnel come off a dungeon?' Tiffany whispered.

'Dunno,' said Frank, trembling in his muddy trainers and scouring the walls for signs of bogeys. 'Dad said old castles sometimes have secret passages, and parts of Snozzle are *really* old – from the time of William the Conkerer, or something. Maybe a prisoner dug it out?'

'Conkerer? Wasn't he that medieval conkers champion?' whispered Tiffany.

But there was no time to contemplate whether prisoners could really dig their way out of deep, terrifying dungeons, or whether William the Conkerer was indeed an olde-worlde conkers champ (clue, nose-pickers: he wasn't. He was allergic to conkers and much preferred apple bobbing),

'cause there came, floating on the air, a strange **SNIFF . .**
. GROWL . . . GRUNT!

I'd like to say it was that weird hedgehog impersonating wolves again, but it wasn't.

'Do you think it's the monster?' whimpered Tiffany.

'My nose isn't tingling, but it must be,' said Frank. 'Maybe we can sneak up on it.' He didn't know where this bravery was coming from. Inside he felt all wibbly-wobbly.

'OK,' said Tiffany, trying to sound just as brave.

As they set off towards the noise, the tunnel started to wind steeply upwards – left, right-left, right – as if they were moving through the stomach of a giant snake. Then, at the next bend, Frank walked straight into a very dusty door. 'OUCH!' He rubbed his head.

'The noise is coming from the other side,' he whispered. It was louder than ever. 'I'll open it after three. Ready? One, two, thr—'

'WAIT!' Tiffany grabbed his elbow. 'We've seen the monster, so we know it looks scary, but do you think it might be . . . you know . . . dangerous?'

Frank froze. She was right. From the moment they'd watched it jump out of the window, they'd only ever thought about finding it. He'd felt drawn to its bogeys, but that didn't mean it was nice. What if it was evil? They simply didn't know whether it was safe.

He gulped. 'I don't think we have a choice. It's my bogey tower, so even if it's dangerous we need to catch it and hide it, to stop it hurting anyone. And if it's nice, well, we still can't have anyone knowing about it.'

Frank's heart did a triple backflip as he imagined his parents seeing it – their horror-struck faces . . . their socks after they'd been sick in them . . . and their announcement that they could never ever love a boy whose disgusting bogey-picking habit had got so out of hand. Then he took a deep breath and gathered all his courage.

'No. We've GOT to open the door!'

Tiffany nodded.

Frank gave it a sharp push.

SNIFF . . . GROWL . . . GRUNT!

The sound engulfed the tunnel.

Frank stepped forward.

Tiffany gasped. 'Careful, the monster might—'

But it was too late.

OOZING BOGEY FLESH

In a whirl of oozing bogey flesh, the monster jumped on Frank and—

STOP!

SORRY, nose-pickers! That's simply not true! I don't know what came over me.

THE MONSTER WAS NOT THERE! Get that image out of your heads.

I repeat:

THE MONSTER WAS NOT THERE!

What *was* there, though, was Frank's muddy face again,

as he poked it back around the door, and said: 'I can't believe it. We're in my bogey cupboard! Look. The door's the back panel.' He pointed. 'It's Mum's snoring we've been hearing!'

'Soaring slugs!' said Tiffany, scrambling after him. 'A secret passage from the dungeon to your bedroom! And you never knew it was there!'

'It must go through the castle walls,' said Frank. 'The dungeon's under the East Wing and my bedroom's in the West!'

'Woah! This is SOOOOO cool!' said Tiffany.

SNIFF ... GROWL ... GRUNT!

'I know,' said Frank. 'But if that's Mum's snoring and the bogey handprints stopped at the gate . . .'

'And *we're* the only ones in your room . . .' added Tiffany. '**Where's** the monster?'

CHAPTER 11 ⁴/₈

WHERE?

WHERE? Or:

* **'Où'** in FRENCH (pronounced *'ooo'*).
* **'Dónde'** in SPANISH (pronounced *'don-day'*).
* **'Wo'** in German (pronounced *'voh'*).
* **'Dove'** in Italian (pronounced *'doh-vay'*).

There you go, now you can impress your friends by saying **'where?'** in four European languages. Though saying **'where?'** won't actually tell you **WHERE** the monster is, will it? So you'd better keep going.

Pffft! You nose-pickers are easily distracted!

WARNING! WARNING!

AS SOON AS YOU TURN THIS
PAGE, YOU WILL FIND OUT
WHERE THE MONSTER IS.
BE **VERY VERY** CAREFUL!

DON'T HOLD IT AGAINST ME
IF IT BITES OFF YOUR HAND,
OR YOUR EAR, OR YOUR BUM,
OR EVEN YOUR BOGEY-FILLED
NOZZLE!

YOU HAVE BEEN
WARNED!

CHAPTER 12

SNOTTY TISSUES

Woah, you're brave!

And look. That page turn has taken you out of Frank's messy bedroom, over Snozzle's leaky rooftops and dishevelled lawns, into an immaculate garden, where (luckily for you) the monster's too busy rifling through a designer bin to notice you're there.

What's it looking for?

Snotty tissues.

Why?

Because **(SPOILER ALERT, SPOILER ALERT)** the

monster eats ... **BOGEYS!** Though don't relax just yet. It might eat human flesh too, it's just too early to tell.

You see, after jumping out of the window into the storm, the monster *had* sheltered behind the dungeon door (where Frank and Tiffany had found the bogeys on the gate). But as soon as the rain had stopped, it had caught a whiff of some **SNOT-FILLED TISSUES**, which had set its stomach a-rumbling and its legs a-trekking towards the delicious aroma – past Snozzle Castle's moat and old orchard, across the crumbly fountain and the broken greenhouse – to a gap in the bushes and NEXT-DOOR'S GARDEN, where the designer bin was bursting with 'em.

Whose bin?

That mean old letter-writer, Willamina Honk!

Why was the bin bursting with 'em?

'Cause she had a cold.

How long had she had it?

About three days!

But stop. You don't need to know the BORING details of Willamina's cold. For this story, you only need to know two things:

1. **Whether she'll find the monster in her garden.**
2. **Why she's writing such nasty letters and why she moved into her ultra-chic, modern house next door to Snozzle Castle in the first place.** (Whoops, sorry, that's two questions in one, isn't it? Oh well!)

I think we'll start with **Number 2** (the two-questions-in-one one),

CHAPTER 13

NUMBER TWO!

Right. Here's **Number 2** (the two-questions-in-one one). It's a short story within this story that happened before this story became an actual story. Got it?

Good. Here goes:

Once upon a time, a girl was born into a very rich family.

Can you guess her name?

It was Mandy Skittlebrow.

Nah, just kidding. It was Willamina. But – here's the thing – her surname wasn't Honk, it was ... **CONK!**

What?

Read on quickly and I'll explain.

So, as I said, her family was rich, but what I meant to say was that they were smack 'em yack 'em rollin' in it – descendants of French king William le Conkerer,[*] with opulent homes all over the globe and bank accounts so full that the only family richer than theirs were their cousins 224 times removed, the royal family. (Or so Willamina had been told all her life.)

Want to know *exactly* how big that bank account was? Grab a calculator, type 1,000,000 (that's one million), then subtract 999,382, then hit equals. Now turn it upside down and read the word:

That's right. It was .

---

* Don't bother looking up William le Conkerer in history books. You won't find him. I, the author, am the world's only expert on this particular French king, so only I know about him. That's how I know Tiffany was wrong – and that William wasn't a conkers champion, but loved apple bobbing. He even won the Battle of Tastings in 1066 by apple bobbing against King Harold, taking the English crown 4,573 pearmains (a medieval apple variety) to 27.

And to say she'd been spoilt would be an understatement.* Whatever she wanted, she got – even as a grown-up.

At age twenty, when Willamina said, 'Papa, I fancy another sports car,' her father replied, 'I'll buy one for you, Tooty Boobles!'

At thirty, when Willamina said, 'Mama, I want another diamond necklace,' her mother cried, 'Let's go shopping, my Patty Poo!'

And at forty, when Willamina declared, 'I want another luxury villa in the south of France,' (she collected villas, mansions, manors and castles, and already had ten of each), her father cooed, *'Tout de suite*, Shnookums!' (which means straight away).

Now I know what you're thinking. *Didn't they ever say NO?*

And the answer is no – EXCEPT ONCE. And that's what this chapter's about.

---

* Don't get me wrong, nose-pickers; not all very wealthy families spoil their kids and turn them into stinkers. There are nice people and nasty people (and sometimes-nasty-and-sometimes-nice people) in all walks of life. Remember that! Life lesson over.

It happened the day after her uncle Henri Conk's funeral, when Willamina, now aged fifty-nine, was lunching at her now-aged parents' lavish manor.

'Papa, now Uncle's no longer with us, I want to add his Snozzle Castle to my collection. Can I have it?'

That's right, nose-pickers. Uncle Henri Conk's castle was none other than Frank's home! Which means Uncle Henri Conk was none other than Frank's dad's biggest fan!

'Sorry, but no, Diddums!' replied her now-wrinkly father.

Willamina almost choked on her dauphinoise potatoes (that's posh tatties baked in cream). She'd obviously heard wrong.

'Your Uncle Henri gifted it to his favourite film director ten years ago.' His voice was wobbly now, as he watched Willamina's pale cheeks glow red. 'What was his name? Pickerty-Boop – or something ridiculous like that. We thought you knew. We haven't owned it for a decade.'

'But I have to have it! William le Conkerer laid the first stone. I'm named after him, aren't I? I want it.'

'I know, Pooky Woo.' He gulped. Even after fifty-nine years, he still couldn't stand seeing his daughter in distress. 'But you know what your uncle was like. When he wasn't claiming mythical creatures like vampires or werewolves were real, he was watching scary movies about them and donating his fortune to' – he shivered – 'penniless artists. But if you want another castle, I'll buy one for you.'

'I don't want a different one. I've got three French ones and seven Scottish ones. I want *that* one! Tell him, Mama.'

'Oh, my Sweet Strawberry. I'm afraid I can't help you,' her mother said in her creaky voice. 'Your father's brother – your odd, mythical-creature- and horror-movie-obsessed uncle –' she gritted her dentures; he'd always been the family embarrassment – 'did indeed give this tiny part of your inheritance away to a pauper filmmaker.'

Her father cleared his throat. 'Well, strictly speaking, Snozzle was in a bad way and, Diddums, you did once tell Henri you'd rather wear second-hand clothes than inherit his ruin.'

But Willamina chose to ignore that last bit. All she'd heard was, 'NO.' And the meaning of it, even at age fifty-nine, was still so strange to her that a new emotion pounded in her bony chest: frustration. Which turned to anger. Which turned to determination.

How dare that oddball artiste stop her getting what was rightfully hers!

She had royal blood.

She was a French Conkerer.

Ohhh, she'd find a way to get that castle back. NO. MATTER. WHAT. And she'd make the Pickled-Poops' lives (or whatever their name was) a misery while she was at it.

And so, dear nose-pickers, THAT's why she was living next to Snozzle Castle and sending nasty letters. When you're spoilt and greedy, there's nothing like a big fat NO to make you want the very things you can't have.

And THAT's why she'd changed her surname from Conk to Honk* - to go incognito, which means *nobody*

knows who you are. And when I say 'nobody', I mean Frank's family, who had no idea that the Honk next door was really a Conk trying to steal their beloved home.

---

*Willamina chose Honk for two reasons: 1) with only one letter change, 'twas easy to remember; 2) she thought it made her sound like the most important person in HONKerty Village.

CHAPTER 13 ⅞

BUMFUZZLE

And so, dear nose-pickers, now you know why Willamina is living next door and being an all-round rotter, it's time for us to fast-forward one whole year to the present, to see if she's going to find the monster in her garden.

Please say the word below:

BUMFUZZLE

(Sorry, but pressing dots is for backwards travel. Forwards time travel only works when you say a silly word, like 'bumfuzzle' - which doesn't mean 'bum hair', by the way. Honestly! Where is your mind? It means 'to confuse'!)

Sorry if I **bumfuzzled** you!

CHAPTER 14

CRASH CLANG DOING!

S plendid.

And so now here we are with Willamina 'Honk', in the present, sitting with her laptop on her knees in her swish all-white lounge, below a portrait of her ancestor William le Conkerer (which she'd had painted especially, 'cause there wasn't a single image of him anywhere in the world).

Why the computer?

'Cause despite her cold and a long day hunting through dusty documents in the Olde Worlde Locale section of

Honkerty Library for information about Snozzle Castle (unsuccessfully, may I add), Willamina was enjoying her new favourite hobby: staying up late to surf i-spy.com, a treasure trove of CCTV recordings from streets all over the country – including Honkerty Village.

'Pfft!' She clicked through the day's videos with mocking lips.

At 2 p.m., before the storm, Mrs Wirrel had worn a ripped coat while walking her five giant poodles in Honkerty Park. A RIPPED COAT! Willamina shuddered. How distastefully pauper-like!

'Urgh!'

At 3 p.m., Squishy the dancing hamster's owner Bo Jacobs had gone home to the tiniest bungalow she'd ever seen. How horrid!

And at 4 p.m., there was Mrs Sniff picking up some small change she'd found on the pavement. Oh, the shame!

Willamina Honk puffed out her bony chest and adjusted her dyed-auburn beehive (not an actual buzzing beehive – a beehive hairdo; it was popular in the olden days, you know – the 1960s). Spying on the village reminded her how much wealthier and better she was than everyone else. It also made her feel powerful, like the royals she was related to 224 times removed – and somehow closer to getting Snozzle Castle back.

She went to the window and gazed longingly at its moonlit silhouette through her designer binoculars – or at least she tried. That thousand-year-old yew tree kept blocking her view to the East Wing. That'd be the first thing to go once she'd got her mitts on the castle.

'A-CHOOOO!' she sneezed. Oh, she HATED having a cold. With a frown, she blew her nose and decided it was time for bed.

In her spotless white bedroom, Willamina clapped her hands – 'CHOP CHOP!' she ordered – and the curtains closed themselves with an automatic hum.

Then she donned a crisp white nightie and curled up under freshly pressed sheets like a wrinkled prawn to read *Spying: The Art of Controlling Your Neighbours* (a 1,023-page book by Will Findout).

'Hmmm,' she smiled as she got to the end of Chapter 4: 'Security Cameras Are Your New Friends'. 'This really is an excellent read.'

CRASH CLANG DOING!

What was that?

She leapt out of bed and grabbed her binoculars.

There was movement by the designer bin, but she couldn't make out what.

'I bet it's those bats again,' she muttered to herself. 'The whole place is riddled with them.'

She threw on her white dressing gown and fluffy white slippers and made her way down the stairs to see who was trespassing.

But the noise hadn't come from the flock of sweet furry bats that often fluttered around her shrubbery. No. It was coming from . . .

Well, you know, don't you?

CHAPTER 15

GOO-GOO-GOOEY!

Willamina's eyes strained through the eerie moonlight.

To the left she saw nothing but her flawless lawn, silver-tinged like a ghostly carpet.

To the right, she saw nothing but her flawless lawn, silver-tinged like a ghostly carpet.

Straight ahead, she saw nothing but— You get the picture. Then she heard a high-pitched gurgle.

'GOO-GOO-GOOEY.'

What on earth made a noise like that? She'd never

heard anything like it.

'I bet it's Mrs Sniff's mog,' she muttered. 'I'll hose it to
high heaven.'

But as she marched to the neatly wound hosepipe, she
spotted a shadow, shaped like a little man, looming at the
bottom of her flawless lawn.

'Argh!' It made her jump.

She quickly took aim with the hosepipe nozzle and
squeezed.

PSSSSHTTTTTT

Water shot through the inky air straight into . . . a tree.

'Croque Monsieur!' she cursed, which means 'cheese
and ham toastie'. Willamina loved to say French words
in homage to her French ancestors, especially when she
was angry. They weren't always right, but she didn't know
that because she was so vain she thought everything she
uttered was always perfect. (For more insult translations,
do check the back of the book.)

It had to be the brat next door, playing a trick after

her last nasty letter. Just last week, she'd seen him throw a Frisbee through the hedge (definitely ON PURPOSE), then sneak in to get it.

'Annoying little *ferry pour Calais!*' Willamina yelped. 'Come out, boy, and face me like a sprout-faced *haricot!*'

'GRRR,' came a sudden low growl from the darkness.

With her hose poised for action, Willamina inched back inside and turned on the kitchen light. A rectangle of yellow streamed on to the patio, with Willamina's elongated shadow in the middle of it.

A fluffy brown bat called Binky flew over it.

PSSSSHTTTTTT

Willamina hosed her to the ground, where she flailed in the wet beyond the shadow.

Ha, that'll warn the brat, Willamina thought.

But then an angry burble filled the air – **'GOO-GOO-GOOEY!'** – and before she knew it, a thick, gloopy-green foot had slid into the light, followed by a gloopy-green body and a gloopy-green face smothered in squidgy **GREEN**

PUSTULES. The top of its domed head had mounds, like a wavy hairdo, and its hands were webbed, like duck's feet, except the webbing was . . . *SAUCISSON SEC!* Was that **GOO?**

All Willamina could think was: *The boy, he's in a costume - probably from one of his father's heinous movies - a swamp monster or something. Yes! That's it. Well, I won't be intimidated!*

She raised the hosepipe to give him a good squirt.

'GOO-GOO-GOOEY,' the boy grunted as he scooped the bat into his hands and helped her flutter into the night.

Willamina squeezed the nozzle.

PSSSHTTTTTT

A jet of water streamed straight into the boy's cheek.

'GRRRRRAAAH!' The boy's face was squelchy and sunken where the water had hit. The costume clearly wasn't waterproof!

'GOO-GOO-GOOEY!' He stuck out an impressively real-looking long pink tongue and blew a big, gloopy raspberry.

The boy was very good at staying in 'swamp monster' character, she had to give him that!

She was just about to raise the hose to teach him another lesson, when suddenly, silently, seven red squirrels appeared, followed by a badger, four barn owls and two foxes. And they all lined up like soldiers, stock-still at the boy's feet – almost as if they were protecting him.

It was deeply, deeply creepy!

Get a grip, Willamina ordered herself, all at once feeling shaky. *They're*

probably just stuffed ... animal-shaped props ... special effects.

But then, as an eerie dolphin cry resounded from somewhere behind her bin (courtesy of Honkerty's weird hedgehog), she felt something she'd never felt before: failing courage.

Her knees buckled.

Her arms went rigid.

Her head folded forward.

And for the first time in her life, she fainted to the floor like a stiff accordion.

CHAPTER 16

FILM PROPS

The birds were singing 'Chattanooga Choo-Choo' in broad daylight by the time Willamina came to. Not that she noticed. Her face was sandwiched between her designer binoculars and a puddle.

How on earth had she got there? Never in all her life ...

She got to her feet and looked up at the castle with her binoculars to check no one had seen her. Then it all came flooding back.

She'd never felt so humiliated. What sort of impoverished weirdos used film props to scare their neighbours? If this was payback for her letters, she was clearly going to have to up her game.

She adjusted her beehive and smoothed her damp nightie.

'They want to play dirty? Then I'll play DIRTIER!' she whispered. 'They want to get one over on me? Then I won't let them! No one beats a Honk— Er . . . a Conk. Er . . . a Honk-Conk!'

And then she remembered the chapter she was reading in her *Spying: The Art of Controlling Your Neighbours* book, and a new, nasty idea popped into her head.

And that, dear nose-pickers, leads us to what happened later that morning.

CHAPTER 17

WHAT HAPPENED LATER THAT MORNING

WWW.I-SPY.COM

HIRED HELP NEEDED

CCTV EXPERIENCE REQUIRED

WELL PAID

Click <u>here</u> for more information

EMAIL: Willamina4ever@Willamina.com

**Billy
Basher**

**Steve
Basher**

CHAPTER 18

ICU

'Your name?'

'Billy Basher, ma'am.'

'Occupation?'

'Co-owner of ICU – your essential CCTV installation company.'

'Experience?'

'A few weeks— Er . . . years at ICU. But we've done all sorts o' other stuff before – pest extermination, bodyguarding, abattoir work, burgl— Ahem . . . retrieving valuables for our employers.'

Willamina smirked. Not only did the beefy man sitting

opposite her in her lounge sound like the perfect candidate for sneaking cameras into Snozzle Castle, but the back of his overalls were expertly embroidered with the company name, ICU, and his long handlebar moustache was wonderfully crumb-free. How inspired she had been to post her advert on her new favourite website, www.i-spy.com. And how quickly they had responded!

'And you?' she said to the skinny man next to him. He too had embroidered overalls and an immaculate brown moustache, though his turned upwards into two fine points. 'You must be Steve Basher?'

'That's right, m'lady. I'm Billy's younger brother and my answers are all the same as his.'

Willamina ticked every box on her requirement list. She thought Steve's reply had been a little short, but generally she was satisfied. 'And you both understand what I need you to do?'

'We do, ma'am,' said Billy, getting out his notebook. 'You want us to install CCTV cameras in Snozzle Castle, because - in your own words - you want to keep an eye on that hideous family of artists. They're up to something. The boy wore a swamp monster costume to trespass in your garden. And their house is really yours. But' – he glanced at his pad to double-check – 'you don't want us to break in and fit them until the coast is clear.'

'That's right.'

'So while we wait for the coast to clear, we'll watch the castle gates on i-spy.com and tell you if we see anything unusual.'

These brothers! thought Willamina. *So beneath me, but so well groomed and good at reading my instructions back to me.*

'And you have your own offices, you say?'

'We do, ma'am. ICU HQ.'

'And you both understand I need you to be the souls of discretion?' she said gravely.

'Of course, ma'am,' said Billy. 'No one's more discreet than a CCTV camera fitter.'

Willamina smiled. 'I'll pay you fifty thousand pounds.'

'Make it a hundred and you're on.'

'Fine,' she said without a moment's pause. 'Twas but a droplet in her gargantuan money ocean. She was stinkin'-winkin' rich and far too revved up to quibble. 'You're hired!'

CHAPTER 19

A FAINT WHIFF OF COD

N ow, I don't know about you, but I think there's something fishy about the Basher brothers.

Sniff the air.

Can you smell it?

A faint whiff of cod?

'Wahoo!' cried Billy, once they'd left Willamina's house and climbed into their ICU van. 'What have I always said, Steve?'

'Never pick your toenails with your teeth?'

'Yes . . . NO! Not that. Our WORK MOTTO.'

'Oh,' said Steve, twiddling his pointy moustache, as he always did when he'd said something silly, which was often. 'Wheeler-dealers always win?'

'That's right, bruv. Look at us – pest exterminating one month, burglaring the next, then – BIM-BAM – stuff falls off a truck and we're working for a moneybags with our own CCTV company! Gawd knows why she thinks that castle's hers! And trespassing in a swamp monster costume!' Billy snorted. 'But who cares? This could be our big break. All we have to do is follow her instructions and Bob's your uncle!'

'OK,' said Steve. 'But Bob's your uncle too.'

'Yeah. But I'm not talking about *our* Uncle Bob, am I? It's just a saying. I meant . . . Oh, never mind. Just drive back to the office while I think about what we'll buy with the easiest HUNDRED THOUSAND POUNDS we've ever earned!' He held up his hand for a high five. 'Put it here, bruv!'

SMACK!

CHAPTER 20

I'VE GOT IT!

'What are we going to do?' said Tiffany, opening the slugs' jar to let them try out a new agility course - tunnels made with tied-together toilet rolls suspended from Frank's bedposts. It was a bit like a wobbly rope bridge and designed to help the slugs' balance.

'I don't know,' said Frank, jumping up and down. As I've already mentioned, jumping helped him think.

It was a full seventeen hours since they'd searched the castle for the monster and ended up back in the bogey cupboard listening to Frank's mum snore. Tiffany had had time to cycle home (so her parents wouldn't notice she'd gone), pop to bed and cycle back again. The monster could be anywhere by now!

Frank picked his nose mid-jump.

It wasn't easy and two little snot balls fell to the floor by Sammy and Violet.

When no thoughts came, he slumped to the floor. His brain felt like fuzz – and not surprisingly: in just one evening, his secret bogey tower had turned into a real-life monster, which they'd lost; he and Tiffany had almost fallen to their deaths in a forbidden dungeon; and they'd discovered a secret passageway through the walls between the East Wing and the West – though it had brought them back to square one in his bedroom. As far as school holidays went, this one took the biscuit – a well-weird biscuit, mind you. One with its own sports team and little biscuit cheerleaders singing, 'RA RA RA'.

'If we're going to catch it, I think we should try and work out what it's like,' he said. 'If I do have a connection with it, maybe I can guess things about it.'

'All right,' said Tiffany. 'What would a bogey monster eat?'

Frank stopped jumping. 'Probably bogeys,' he said, though the words *human flesh* also popped into his head. He hoped it was just his nerves talking.

'Bogeys? Wouldn't that be like it was eating itself?'

'Not really,' Frank answered thoughtfully. 'If it leaves a trail of bogeys when it moves, it'd need replenishing.'

'That figures,' said Tiffany. 'What about drink?'

'Well, not water. Water washes bogeys away.' Frank knew this without even thinking. *What's thicker than water?* he asked himself. 'Slug goo, maybe?'

'What's its favourite colour?'

'I don't know. Green. That's a silly question.'

'Not if it's attracted to things that are green.'

'Oh yeah,' Frank replied. 'Well I think it'd like green and black – the black would remind it of nostrils.'

'And where do you think it is now?'

Frank closed his eyes. He tried to visualize where the

monster might be hiding, but his nose wasn't tickling. All he saw were flashes from his own memory – of the first two bogeys he'd ever wiped in his cupboard, and then of the pile that had gradually grown into a fully fledged bogey tower that had done nothing but stand perfectly still and cause no trouble at all. *How simple life had been until yesterday afternoon!*

'Well, if it does eat bogeys,' and *human flesh*, his mind added, 'then my guess is the village. That's where there's the most people. And where there are people, there are bogeys . . .' And *human flesh.*

'Which is a bad thing,' said Tiffany, as if reading his mind. 'If it *is* dangerous, it might hurt someone.'

'We need to find it fast,' said Frank. 'But it'll take for ever to search the whole village. And what if it's hiding in someone's house? We can't just knock on doors saying, "Excuse me, can we come and hunt for our bogey monster?"'

Frank stared at the slugs. Slim and Peach were racing along the toilet-roll rope bridge (Peach in the tunnel and

Slim on top, '**MEEP!**'), but Sammy and Violet were still by the snot balls that had fallen out of Frank's nose earlier. It looked like a little trail.

Frank gasped.

'I've got it! If we can't find the monster ourselves, we'll get it to come to us.'

CHAPTER 21

SLOP SLOP SLOP!

Nose-pickers, what would you do to get a monster to come to you?

Can you guess what Frank decided to do?

I'll give you a clue:

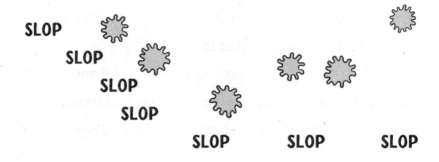

SLOP SLOP SLOP SLOP

SLOP SLOP SLOP

That's right! He decided to make a bogey trail.

The idea was that he and Tiffany would leave the monster a trail to eat and follow between the village centre and Frank's bogey cupboard – then they'd ... Well, they'd think about what to do later.

They'd start in the cupboard, go back through the dungeon, and (making sure Mum and Dad didn't see them) head across the castle grounds to end in the village – making an extra-long version of the snot trail Frank had followed the night before, except this time the *monster* would be following *his* bogeys. They couldn't be sure it would work (what if it didn't eat snot after all?), but neither friend had a better idea.

And so off they went – through the tunnel and dungeon, across the garden, out the gates, past Willamina's house and Mrs Sniff's after that and into the village, where it was a . . .

SLOP SLOP HERE
AND A SLOP SLOP THERE
HERE A SLOP
THERE A SLOP
EVERYWHERE A SLOP SLOP, until . . .

'Stop,' Tiffany whispered, as they headed down Sneaky Beak Lane.

Frank took his finger out of his nose.

POP!

Mrs Sniff was walking slowly in their direction. The friends dropped down and pretended to tie their shoelaces. They'd found that shoelace-tying was the best way to avoid drawing attention to themselves as they'd gone along their trail – past Mrs Wirrel and her five giant poodles, past Bo Jacobs with Squishy his dancing hamster (fully recovered from the storm episode, I'm pleased to say, and performing flamenco), and past friendly Gary Plonk the farmer, who'd shouted, 'Hellooo!'

Right now, Frank welcomed the pause. After slopping

on the school railings and in Hooter Alley's bushes, they'd pretty much covered everywhere they needed and his nostrils were beginning to hurt. He definitely wasn't used to extracting so many bogeys in such a short amount of time.

'Your nose is pink,' said Tiffany, looking out for him, as best friends do. 'Shall I take over?'

'Yeah, that'd be great,' said Frank. 'This way.'

SLOP

SLOP

SLOP

'**Gooliemaloolie**, that last one was big,' he cried admiringly, as Tiffany wiped a whopper of a booger on to the base of a fence panel.

'Thanks!' Tiffany laughed.

Then they carried on all the way down Snout Back Alley – **SLOP** – and back to Snozzle Castle – **SLOP** – laughing and snorting along the way. And somewhere, between their giggling and their nose-picking (just for fun this time), Frank realized it was the first time they'd

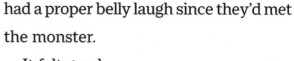

had a proper belly laugh since they'd met the monster.

It felt good.

It made finding the creature not seem so impossible.

And so, as Lucy Longlegs the cabaret spider sang a haunting tune about marshmallows somewhere high up in the deserted East Wing rafters, it was with a light heart and a spring in their step that Frank and Tiffany went back to his bedroom to wait and see if their plan would work.

CHAPTER 22

REEETCH!!!

'**B**illy, Billy! Look here,' cried Steve Basher, sitting in the ICU office, his eyes riveted to Snozzle Castle's gates as he played back the last hour of video footage on i-spy.com. 'Those kids. Ugh! That one's picking his nose and wiping it on the pavement.'

'Well, I've seen some things in my time,' said Billy, putting down a flatscreen he was installing on the wall, 'but never that. It's disgusting. **BRRRRRR.**' His droopy moustache shimmered like a curtain as he shivered. 'Do you know what, bruv?'

'What?'

'I hate bogeys. I mean, I might scratch my bum from time to time. But have you ever seen me pickin'?'

'Never!'

'Exactly. I mean, look at those kids. It's disgusting. It makes me want to retch. **REEEETCH!** Gawd! I just did!' He sat down. 'We've seen some bad things in our time, haven't we? Dead rats with stinky entrails, that zoo camel who gobbed in your mouth, and remember that three-headed fish when we burgled that animal testing lab? **BRRR!** But a bogey? I suppose I can tolerate my own, at a STRETCH, but other people's?'

'You can tolerate your own bogeys if they're stretched?' said Steve, his eyes crossing as he tried to look at his own nose.

'No, I said "at a stretch", Steve. Gawd! Never mind.'

He took a screenshot of Frank and Tiffany and hit print on the computer. 'Come on. The Honkster said to tell her if we see anything unusual and bogey-wiping on the pavement isn't normal, is it? We should probably show her! **REEEETCH!**'

BOGEY ALERT!
BOGEY ALERT!

Nose-pickers, watch out.

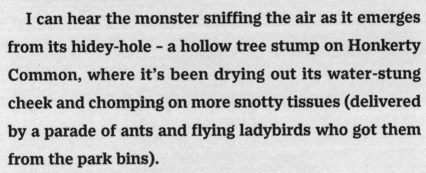

I can hear the monster sniffing the air as it emerges from its hidey-hole – a hollow tree stump on Honkerty Common, where it's been drying out its water-stung cheek and chomping on more snotty tissues (delivered by a parade of ants and flying ladybirds who got them from the park bins).

SNIFF! SNIFF!

Maybe it's smelt Frank and Tiffany's bogey trail?

Or maybe it's smelt the glob-nuggets up your own hairy hooter?

Either way, it's on the move, so keep your eyes peeled.

YOU HAVE BEEN WARNED.

CHAPTER 23

A TRAP

Frank looked at the clock. With every passing minute, he could feel the excitement of having completed the snot trail morphing into a big ball of worry that tore at his chest.

Tiffany had put Sammy, Violet, Peach and Slim in an empty washing-up bowl so they could make a vat of slime, in the hope that the monster did indeed drink slug goo and that once it saw how much there was, it would be less likely to eat them!

And Frank had barricaded his bedroom door with a

chair, in case Mum or Dad tried to get in while the monster was there. It wasn't much, but anything was better than mulling over the questions in his brain:

Why hasn't the monster arrived yet?

Maybe it doesn't eat bogeys?

Maybe it hasn't found the trail?

Is it asleep?

Or has someone already found it and killed it? Or worse . . . has it found them?

'Frank?' said Tiffany, snapping him out of his thoughts. 'It's five o'clock. I'm going to have to cycle home soon. It's Great-gran's birthday, remember. She's one hundred and three today, so I can't miss the party. And my cousin's sharing my room so I can't sneak out.'

'Gooliemaloolie!' Frank had forgotten. Panic rose as he realized he'd soon be waiting for the bogey monster alone.

'*Fraaaank?*' It was Mum singing down the hall, while accidentally knocking over Dad's life-size skeleton prop (now an ornament on a stand) from one of his films. 'Whoops! Er . . . Your dinner'll be ready in about fifteen minutes, OK?'

'OK!' he shouted back, then turned to Tiffany. 'What am I going to do? I can't leave the room empty while I eat my tea. What if the monster comes when I'm not here?'

'We could make a trap!' Tiffany suggested. 'Just to keep it contained. Not to hurt it. That way if it does turn up while you're out, you'll find it when you get back.'

Frank wasn't sure – if it got stuck in a trap it might make a noise, plus they only had fifteen minutes – but he couldn't think of anything better, and Tiffany's enthusiasm was always catching. So, he rifled through his chest of drawers and pulled out his Frisbee, an old yo-yo, an extra-long straw and a set of football goal nets still in their box (Frank preferred bogey balls to ball games). 'Do you think we can use any of these?'

'Maybe ... yes.' Tiffany looked thoughtful for a second, then her cheeks started glowing, which usually meant she was having a brilliant moment.

And sure enough, in a flash, she'd made the yo-yo and the Frisbee into a pulley and attached it to one of the nets, which Frank then helped her hang over the secret door.

'Gooliemaloolie! It actually looks good,' he said.

'Thanks, it's all down to my slug-agility-course-making practice!' Tiffany grinned, then popped the extra-long straw into the bucket of slug goo below the net, so it could be sucked up like a milkshake.

Sammy, Violet, Peach and Slim did a little boogie in their slime.

And then the friends found themselves laughing again, not because Tiffany had said something funny or because the slugs looked silly – though they did, especially when Slim did an overenthusiastic backflip and landed on Peach's eye tentacles – but because they were nervous.

They were nervous that:
* they'd be found out
* their plan wouldn't work
  OR WORSE
* their plan WOULD work, and the monster would turn out to be a horrible beast that ate them alive

A thoughtful expression fell over Tiffany's face. 'It's

made of your bogeys. And you're my best friend. I can't believe anything that came from you would be evil.'

'And your slugs helped stick the tower together,' Frank added. 'Maybe something made from friendship can't be bad?'

Frank blushed. Tiffany stared at her shoes. They'd never said anything soppy like that before.

'Can you leave the slugs?' said Frank. 'They can carry on making slime while you're gone.'

'Yes.' Tiffany leant over the washing-up bowl. 'They must have already made enough to fill a couple of teacups. I'll get my dad to drop me off here after breakfast tomorrow. If the monster appears, don't let it escape.'

Frank didn't know quite how he'd do that, but he nodded.

'Your dinner's ready,' Dad called down the corridor.

'Good luck,' said Tiffany.

'Coming,' Frank shouted.

Then, from the front door, came the *snap* of the letter box. Someone had posted an envelope.

CHAPTER 24

THE LONGEST DINNER EVER

'**W**HA-KAK!'

It was the sound of Frank choking on a baked bean as Mum read out a line from the letter: '. . . your revolting son and his friend wiping bogeys outside my house . . .'

'**WHA-KAK!**'

Dad thumped Frank's back. The bean flew out of his mouth, whizzed over the tea-stained table – **FLOOSH** – and cannonballed through the gap between the salt shaker and the fruit bowl.

'It's a goal!' shouted a fruit fly, before being bowled over by the bean.

'Is this true?' asked Mum disappointedly.

She was talking to Frank, not the fly (he was unconscious and wouldn't have known the answer anyway).

Frank took a gulp of water. 'It w-wasn't us,' he stuttered. But his insides were screaming, **HEEEEEEELLLPPPPPP!** *This is it. Mum and Dad are going to find out and stop loving me.*

'Well, it looks like you were!' She thrust a printout of the Bashers' screenshot under his nose. It showed Frank having a fully fledged poke around.

'I might have picked a bit, but I didn't wipe it anywhere,' he lied again. Not as convincingly as he would have liked. His finger was halfway up his nostril and he could feel the colour draining from his freckly face.

'Er ... Frank!' said Dad.

'Sorry.' POP!

'And what's this about you trespassing in her garden wearing a swamp monster costume?' said Mum.

WHAAAAAAT? The MONSTER! *She had to be talking about the monster! Of all the places for it to go ...* **GOOLIEMALOOLIE!** *Was that where it was hiding now?*

'I didn't ...' Frank squirmed like a worm on a hook. He wanted to cry ... and pick his nose ... then cry some more ... and pick his nose harder.

'My darlings! My darlings!' Dad put his arm around Mum's and Frank's shoulders. 'Look what that woman is doing to us! You might have a wandering index finger, Frank, but we know you wouldn't do anything THAT disgusting, would you?'

'**GAAAAAAAAAAH!**' He couldn't form a word.

'And the idea of you trespassing in her garden late at night, dressed up as a swamp monster ...' Dad stifled a laugh as he read the rest of the paragraph, 'with prop animals from one of my *"despicable films"* . . . is, well, hilarious! I should put that in a movie script! She's clearly deranged – plus, I'm sure it's illegal to take photos of kids in the street.'

'Oh, you're right,' said Mum, joining in with a laugh. 'It's just, between the castle's upkeep, our money problems and the storm damage' – she got up to stir the custard on the hob (it was burning) – 'things are bad enough without next door weighing in again. I'm sorry, Frank. You're a good *booooooy*,' she sang, trying to be cheerful again, before adding in a very high, dramatic soprano voice, 'Thank *gooooodneeeess*. I don't know how we'd *cooooope* if you weren't.'

Frank fake-smiled, but his guilt level whooshed off the scale from ninety-nine out of a hundred to twenty-seven thousand million trillion. This was starting to feel like the longest dinner ever.

Emotions whirled round his head. **GUILT** about the lying and the bogey-wiping, **FEAR** that his parents would uncover the truth and stop loving him (or that Honk-bum

– as he and Tiffany called Willamina – would discover the truth), and **TERROR** that he'd released a bloodthirsty monster into the world AND that his trail wouldn't work. Or worse. That it WOULD.

GUILT ...

       TERROR   **FEAR**

    GUILT   **TERROR**

  FEAR   **WHOOSH!**   **FEAR**

    TERROR   **GUILT**

      FEAR   **TERROR**

        GUILT

He needed to get back to his room.

'Can I leave the table, please?' he asked, sweating. 'I'm feeling really . . . tired.'

'It's only six o'clock! And you haven't had any pudding.'

'I know,' said Frank, frowning at the burnt bits in the custard. 'But I really need to lie down.'

'All right, love.' Mum kissed him on his head and flattened his ginger curls. 'Gosh, you are clammy, and you do look peaky. I'm not surprised after all this Honk malarkey. I'll

save you some custard and check in on you later.'

Frank didn't need telling twice. He dashed off down the corridor, slipped into his room and closed the door carefully behind him.

Panting, he checked on the slugs. Slim and Violet were having a swimming race in their slime. Sammy and Peach were taking it in turns to slide down the long drinking straw.

Frank drew his tatty curtains and turned off the light as a precaution, so his parents wouldn't see the trap if they came in. There was no point barricading himself inside. Mum and Dad would always check on him if they thought he was ill, and blocking the door would only cause extra trouble. He just hoped the monster wouldn't show up while they were awake.

Frank lay back on his bed and watched the fiery light of the setting sun pierce the holes in his curtains and dance on the ceiling like butterflies, which was exactly what he had in his stomach when he thought about the monster.

CHAPTER 24 & A BIT

CHOCOLATE ALERT!

Do you have butterflies too, nose-pickers? I do. 'Cause listen:

RUSTLE RUSTLE RUSTLE SQUELCH SQUEKCH STOMP!

Can you hear it? It's the monster on the move again, down Snout Back Alley I think.

And look! **SLUUUUUURP LIIIIIIICK – it's gobbling SNOT SLOPS!**

You know what that means, don't you?

CHOCOLATE ALERT!!! CHOCOLATE ALERT!

QUICK! EAT SOME RIGHT *NOOOOOOOOW*!

A BIG HULKING BALLY-WALLY BALL should do it. Or any other of your preferred sorts . . . Just be FAST! The next bit's VERY **VERY** scary, so, you might be too frightened to eat.

CHAPTER 25

SPLASH!

Did you know that stress can make you sleepy?

It can. Just this morning when I realized I'd run out of Bally-Wally Balls: **SPLAT!** I dozed off in my bowl of cereal. And a similar thing happened to Frank. He was so anxious about the monster that he dropped off while lying on his bed, fully dressed, in the dark. He didn't snort milk or wake up with soggy cornflakes on his eyelids, but he did snooze for a long time, not stirring when Mum checked on him (don't worry, she didn't see the trap), and only waking when he heard a loud . . .

SNIFF ... GROWL ... GRUNT!

Frank sat bolt upright and glanced at his clock. It read 3.13 a.m.

SNIFF ... GROWL ... GRUNT!

He kicked himself for having fallen asleep.

SNIFF ... GROWL ... GRUNT!

He switched on his bedside light, then dived under his covers, making a spy tunnel through his quilt to watch his secret cupboard door for signs of the monster. He'd never felt so scared.

SNIFF ... GROWL ... GRUNT!

Then it dawned on him.

It was Mum snoring AGAIN!

Frank pressed his ear to the wall to check. Sure enough, there was Mum's familiar drone. *Fancy being caught out twice!* He shook his head, thinking back to his adventures in the tunnel the night before. At least this meant Mum and Dad were still asleep.

He peered over his bed at the slugs. They were zonked out in their gloopy pool - and understandably so. They'd almost filled the entire bowl with slime.

But the monster wasn't here yet, and it had been hours since he and Tiffany had left the trail. Frank just had to face facts: their plan had failed. He almost felt relieved. The thought of facing the monster alone gave him the collywobbles.

But then:

SPLASH!

A blob of slug goo flew out of the washing-up bowl and splatted on Frank's cheek. The slugs were hauling themselves over the side of the bowl. Sammy, Violet and Peach were trembling, and Slim seemed to be keeping watch, his eye tentacles like quivering periscopes. It was as if the slugs knew something Frank didn't.

Then his nose tickled.

CHAPTER 26

A GREEN-BROWN HAND

Frank held his breath as a green-brown hand crept silently around the side of the bogey cupboard door.

A stubby, bobbly thing that thinned into transparent green webs between a thumb and two stodgy fingers. The same two digits Frank used for bogey picking!

A waterfall of thoughts washed over him.

* The monster's here!
* Our trail has worked!
* We were right. It eats bogeys!
* Will it eat me, too?

✳ **Tiffany, I wish you were here!**

✳ **AAAAAAAARGH!**

Every muscle in his body wanted to run. But all he could do was watch as the webbed hand terrifyingly turned into a bobbly arm, attached to a crinkly bogey body, with short legs and a neckless head shaped like a dome – just like his tower. Where the monster's face had once looked slimy, it now seemed dry and cracked, with a deep hollow in one of its flaky cheeks. Eruptions of brown-green bogeys bordered vivid yellow-green eyes that blinked as they adjusted to the light in his bedroom. It was much stranger than Frank remembered.

The monster quivered, then . . .

WHOOSH!

In a snap, the pulleys and string of Frank and Tiffany's trap were set into motion and the net dropped straight over the monster.

'GOO-GOO-GOOEY,'

it burbled, battling against the mesh. Its mouth was huge, with a pink tongue lolling like a ragdoll between peg-like teeth. Whenever it rubbed its flesh up against the net, its bogey skin stuck to the fibres – a crust here, a sliver there. The net was soon covered in crumbly snot.

Then suddenly, as if the monster had realized it was losing bits of itself, it stopped struggling and looked straight at Frank.

Frank wanted to scream, but gasped air like a goldfish instead, locked in a gaze with the monster.

How big and gloopy its eyes were – with no whites, just wide black pupils floating in yellow-green ooze.

'H-hello,' Frank whispered, though his brain screamed, **GET OUT. NOOOOW! BEFORE IT EATS YOU!!!**

'A-are you thirsty?'

Where were these niceties coming from? It must have been his nerves.

The monster stood, staring at him.

Suddenly, as if prompted by Frank's question, Slim came catapulting off Violet's back in a triple somersault – **WHEEE**

– and landed in the bowl, pushing the extra-long straw towards the monster's mouth. The monster immediately started sucking up the slime. Frank had been right. It did drink slug goo, and it was clearly very thirsty. But would it be enough to stop it from gobbling him too?

Slim oozed back to the other slugs. They all did little high fives with their eye tentacles. **MEEP!**

Then the monster did something wholly unexpected. It spat out the straw, looked up at Frank and stretched out a tacky finger to point at the net.

It was telling him to take it off.

CHAPTER 27

HOOK. PULL . . .

'**B**aa,' Frank murmured. '**Baa. Baa.**'

He knew he sounded like a sheep, but he couldn't get his words out. Plus, he didn't know what to say.

'**Gaa. Gaa,**' mimicked the monster quietly, pointing to the net again.

Frank caught himself chuckling. Not because it was funny, but because he couldn't believe he was talking to it.

Frank looked into the monster's eyes again. It was foul and terrifying, but somewhere in the middle of its greeny-yellowy eye ooze he saw distress. It reminded him of a puppy looking for its mum. Or – dare he say it – a bogey looking for its creator.

'OK,' Frank said, trembling.

Not wanting to get too close, he grabbed a stick from the wall by his wardrobe and moved it slowly towards the net.

The monster stood quite still.

HOOK.

PULL . . .

And the net was off.

The creature began to gurgle. Then – **GOOLIEMALOOLIE!** – its face distorted into a horrifying grimace, all peggy teeth and bobbly tongue, and it suddenly looked wild and dangerous. It stepped towards Frank.

'Don't eat me,' Frank croaked, holding the stick tightly.

The slugs huddled into a ball and rolled out of the way under the bed. **MEEEEEEEEEP!**

The monster plunged its head into the washing-up bowl, coating its face in slug slime. It cupped more slime in its webbed hands and rubbed under its arms, over its webbed fingers and toes, and into the holes in its cheek. Then it grabbed the bowl and tipped the last few drops of goo over its head, before wiggling its knobbly body like a hula-hoop dancer and giving a satisfied sigh. **'AHHHHHH!'**

Frank nearly fell over backwards. The monster's surface was glistening again, and its face was no longer flaky or hollow. It had had a slug-goo makeover.

And then, as it turned towards Frank, the corners of its mouth lifted upwards, just like a smile.

Frank let out a nervous giggle and put down the stick. Then instinct told him to pick his nose.

SLOP

He wiped a bogey on the bedpost, then another on the tattered carpet. Sure enough, the monster started to follow the trail, and soon it was standing next to him in the middle of the room.

CHAPTER 28

FOLLOW ME!

Cautiously, with his heart beating a trillion zillion miles an hour, Frank held out his hand.

Sammy, Violet, Peach and Slim crept out of their hiding place to watch, as the monster hesitantly lifted a webbed finger to touch Frank's index. To Frank's surprise, the monster didn't feel cold and soft, but warm and hard, like human skin, just with a bit more slime. It felt rather like the inside of his nose, which he supposed made sense.

As Frank wrapped his fingers around the monster's hand, the monster shivered and closed its eyes, and Frank realized two things:

1. **He was no longer scared of it.**
2. **Just because it was a monster, didn't mean it was evil.**

It had only been alive for about thirty-four hours. How terrifying it must have been, being a bogey tower one minute, then a living, breathing monster the next – a monster that Frank and Tiffany had screamed at. And who knew what Honk-bum had done to it when she'd mistaken it for him – or what else had happened to it since it had jumped out of his bedroom window. In fact, standing there, holding its hand, he could feel such gentleness pouring out of it. It was as if he was seeing the creature in a whole new light. A soft yellow light, to be exact.

Just like the light suddenly **SEEPING THROUGH THE CRACK UNDER HIS BEDROOM DOOR!**

Frank gasped. Mum's snoring had stopped, and he recognized the shuffle of her novelty violin slippers moving down the fully lit corridor.

Frank grabbed his sheet from his bed for the second

time in two days, flung it over the creature and turned off his bedroom light. The monster seemed to understand because it stood motionless.

BRUUUUP!

It was the burp of Snozzle Castle's loo flushing.

Mum and Dad's bedroom door clicked shut.

Phew. They'd not been caught this time, but it would be too risky for the monster to stay in Frank's room much longer.

'I'm going to have to find somewhere safe for you to hide,' he whispered, wishing he and Tiffany had thought things through more. He turned his light back on, removed the sheet and popped the slugs into their jar. 'But where?'

He couldn't put the monster in the bogey cupboard, because it was linked to the dark and dangerous dungeon, which led outside, so the creature might get hurt or wander out and get lost again. And he couldn't keep it in the tiny West Wing, 'cause Mum and Dad would find it in five seconds flat – which only left one place.

Can you guess where, nose-pickers?

That's right.

THE ABANDONED, FORBIDDEN EAST WING.

'Follow me.'

1. Cross-eyed gargoyle
2. Holey roof
3. Gloopy green moat
4. Mum and Dad's room
5. Toilet that goes buurpp!
6. Frank's room
7. Uphill tunnel
8. To the kitchen
9. Spiders' cabaret
10. Abandoned East Wing
11. Forbidden dungeon
12. Rickety bell tower
13. Dribbling chops
14. Overgrown gardens
15. Big black hole

CHAPTER 29

A TRIPLE SLAP

The East Wing's spooky entrance hall had gaping holes in the marble floors and jungles of spiderwebs in the beamed ceilings. Frank should have felt frightened; he'd never been there before. But strangely, with the monster by his side, he wasn't.

'AHHHH-AHHHH my Arachnid Angel!' came a faint noise from the rafters. Lucy's husband Lakeland Longlegs was swinging from a thread for the cabaret's new musical, *Incy-Wincy Phantom of the Opera*.

The monster looked up with a **'GURGAHHHH-AHHHH'**

noise that sounded like he was trying to join in, but Frank didn't notice. His eyes were too busy darting over the peeling green walls, dusty mirrors, boarded-up windows and holey floor, looking for a comfy, non-dangerous space for the monster.

There were huge wooden panels on the far wall where big old portraits hung skew-whiff. In one, a very old man dressed as a king had a very dainty nose.

I wonder if he picked it? Frank thought.

HOW DARETH THEE, PEASANT, the portrait seemed to say. I WOULDST NEVER HAVE PICKED MINE OWN HONKER. BEHOLD THE TROUBLE IT DIDETH GET THEE INTO.

Frank glanced at the monster.

The portrait had a point.

Frank shone the torch through a grand, sculpted doorway into the next room, where weird silhouettes danced in the torchlight over the red, threadbare carpet like a creepy shadow puppet show. The room was long and narrow, with an alcove full of old books and a saggy settee set in front of a massive old stone fireplace covered in carvings of werewolf heads. All were snarling, with sharp teeth, but some had bows between their ears and one, at the top, wore a bowler hat. It was well wacky and quite unlike anything Frank had seen before, even in Dad's films.

'Try this as a bed,' Frank said, pointing to the settee.

The monster leapt on to it, causing dust to billow upwards and tickle Frank's nostrils.

'AH-AH . . . CHOOO!'

Frank blew his nose on a tissue from his trouser pocket. Immediately, the monster took the tissue and swallowed it down.

Frank quickly realized that he and Tiffany were going to have to get nose-picking again, and fast. Not only were they going to have to feed the creature, but they were going to have to feed it a lot. Frank had an old lunchbox back in his bedroom. Perhaps they could fill that with bogeys?

'So, what do you think?' Frank asked, turning his attention back to the monster. 'Is this room OK?'

But before Frank could get an answer, there was a cacophony of squeaks as a swarm of bats swooped down from the rafters, flitting around him like a giant cape. A **SWISH** this way, a **SWASH** that. **A SLAP** on his forehead. A triple **SLAP** on his bum!

'ARGH!' Frank waved his hands from head to bottom for protection. But it was no use. The bats were **ALL OVER HIM!**

CHAPTER 30

'GANGOO!'

Frank dropped to the ground in a ball, the slug jar tight to his chest.

'**GOO-GOO-GOOEY!**' The monster's green bobbly body suddenly emerged from a cloud of black wings to stand over Frank. '**GRRRRR.**'

It wasn't a nasty growl - more of a gurgle - but the bats clearly knew what it meant. They stopped diving and swooping, and fluttered back up to the rafters.

'Thanks,' Frank said, slowly lifting his head.

'Goo,' said the monster. But not to Frank. It was talking

to a small brown bat hanging upside-down from one of its knobbly green fingers, as if they knew each other.

And that's because they did.

Remember the bat Willamina sprayed with her hosepipe?

Well, it wasn't her.

Nah, I'm only joking. It was Binky all right. And both the monster and Binky seemed very pleased to see each other. The monster was stroking Binky's little furry tummy and Binky was cuddling the monster's webbed finger with her wings.

Of course, Frank didn't know anything about the bat being saved from Willamina's hosepipe. He just stood there with his mouth wide open – until a blob of bat poo fell from the ceiling on to his cheek, and then he closed it fast.

'So, would you like to stay in here?' he asked the monster again, after a moment, wiping the poop off with his sleeve. The room was dark and narrow, after all. If Snozzle Castle had nostrils, this would be one of them.

'**Goo**,' said the monster with a nod.

'**Eek**,' said Binky in agreement.

Frank immediately made the monster a bed on the dusty settee (with a moth-eaten blanket he'd found stuffed behind a cushion), which caused him to sneeze a few more times, much to the monster's delight.

SLURP.

'**Gangoo**,' said the monster, unexpectedly.

'Y-you're welcome,' Frank replied, hardly believing his ears.

They smiled at each other again, and Frank got a squishy feeling inside, as if something important had just happened.

And that's because it had. He and the monster had become friends.

And Binky had become a friend too, as Frank found out when she flew on to his ear and hung upside down to nibble his shoulder.

And the slugs had become friends with the monster *and* Binky, as Frank discovered when he unscrewed their jar.

And in that moment, everybody in the forbidden East Wing was friends with each other.

And next door, even Willamina smiled, though hers was evil because she'd finally found what she'd been looking for in some documents she'd stolen from Honkerty Village Library's Olde Worlde Locale section.

And Tiffany woke up for a second after Great-gran's party with a grin on her face.

And the Basher brothers chuckled for seemingly no reason as they wearily watched the castle gates on i-spy.com in their office.

And I bet you're smiling now too, aren't you? You see?

That's what happens when nice things happen.

Well, hold that thought, 'cause things aren't going to stay happy for long. Though you'll probably be all right in this chapter. Probably. I think. Oh, I don't know.

Frank peeled back a thin sliver of newspaper from the blacked-out window. A line of purplish light shone in. 'Monster?' he said, making a mental note to find the creature a name.

'**GOO?**' it replied.

'It's almost sunrise, I've got to go. But I'll be back later with some bogeys. And Tiffany, my best friend.'

'**GOO-GOOEY?**' the monster asked.

'Don't worry, Tiffany's cool,' Frank promised. 'She's already seen you.'

The monster shook its head. It wasn't talking about Tiffany. It pointed at the slugs and went '**GLUG-GLUG-GLUG.**'

'You want them to stay to make more goo drink?' Frank asked.

The monster nodded. Sammy, Violet, Peach and Slim immediately slunk over to the monster's foot, where they sat, happy to help. That was settled, then.

Waving goodbye, Frank set off back home to the West Wing, locking the door behind him, before sneaking back to his bedroom, removing all evidence of the trap and jumping into bed, where a strange film of everything that had just happened played through his head.

GOOLIEMALOOLIE! Wait 'til he told Tiffany!

CHAPTER 31

JUST ONE MORE THING

Over at ICU HQ, Willamina Honk sauntered victoriously into the Bashers' office, with designer heels on her feet and a blue file in her bony hands.

Boy, did she look smug.

Boy, did she look haughty.

Boy, did the brothers jump as she slapped the file on to the table, sending a gust of stale air through their lavish moustaches.

'I've done it. I've worked out how to clear the coast.' She reapplied her red lippie and patted her beehive. She felt more powerful than the day she'd ordered Mama and Papa to fire the gardener for planting red rather than yellow tulips! 'Are these the cameras?'

'They are, ma'am,' said Billy, a ball of energy suddenly rising from his sluggish chest as he realized the boring bits (staring at Snozzle's gates on i-spy.com) were finally over and they were getting closer to their pay cheque.

'Good.' She opened the file and unfolded a dusty square of paper. 'Now, here's a plan of Snozzle Castle, which I stole from Honkerty Village Library.'

'Stole?' Billy almost fell off his seat. 'Very impressive, ma'am.'

'Thank you.' Willamina glowed with her own cleverness. 'It shows every room in the house – the West Wing, where the family live; the East Wing, where they don't. Which means every room you're going to install the cameras.'

'Righto,' said Billy. 'West Wing and East Wing. But how will we know when the coast is clear?'

'With this.' Willamina showed Billy an envelope. 'I shall post it through their letter box now. It's a letter requesting that the ENTIRE Pickerty-Boop family come to my house today at ten o'clock to discuss a big problem I've noticed at Snozzle Castle. You will hide in your van outside, and wait until the family are on their way to see me.' At this moment, Willamina's face took on a wicked smirk (something known in the wicked-smirking business as a 'wicksmirk'). 'And that's when you'll find a way into the castle to install the cameras.'

'Got it,' the brothers cried.

'Just one more thing. You mentioned you'd once worked as pest exterminators?'

'That's right, ma'am.'

'Good.' She wick-smirked again. 'Because once you've finished planting the cameras, I need you to catch some rats.'

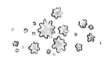

CHAPTER 32

MY APOLOGIES!

My sincere apologies, nose-pickers. The next paragraph is boring. REALLY BORING. But I have no choice, so here goes:

Willamina posted the letter, then went back to her flawless white house where she would receive her visitors. At 9 a.m., the Bashers parked the ICU van in a little alley close to the rusty gates of Snozzle Castle, making sure it was well hidden behind some bushes, then waited for the family to leave and the coast to clear.

There. It's over.

Perhaps now would be a good time to pick your

nozzle. Or as I always like to say, dig for snozgold, or extract a chumpclump, or if it won't budge, a clingenglob. Or perhaps you could invent some bogey terms of your own?

I'll start you off:

* **SNOZZLE CRUMPET** - a big round crusty one, like a crumpet
* **SNEEZE BABY** - a small sloppy one that whizzes out when you breathe hard or sneeze
* **CAKEY FLAKEY** - a stubborn flaky one that won't come off your finger even when you rub

Or perhaps you could just read on . . .

CHAPTER 33

YOURS BLAH BLAH BLAH

'**A**re you sure you're feeling better this morning?' Dad asked, plopping the post on the kitchen table next to Frank, before pottering with a second-hand lens he'd bought for his camera.

'*Ye-e-e-e-e-e-e-ees*. You've hardly touched your cornflakes,' sang Mum, while practising her daily scales in the music area (which was really just a piano in the corner between the fridge and the settee).

'I'm fine,' Frank replied, shovelling in a mouthful to make his point.

And it was true.

After his night with his new bogey friend, he'd woken up with a big grin on his face and now he just couldn't stop daydreaming about all the wonderful things they would do together.

He wanted to:

* **Take it picnicking. It was hay-fever season, so with everyone sneezing and snotting everywhere he might not have to pick his nose so much.**

* **Take it cycling. The monster's legs were too short for pedalling, but it could sit in Tiffany's bike basket. And they knew a lovely secluded route through Honkerty Forest where there was always lots of slug goo.**

* **Show it where he and Tiffany went to school. It couldn't go inside, of course, but at least it would know where the friends would be spending most of their time once term started again.**

Frank knew he couldn't do any of these things just yet, but he'd rarely felt more excited . . . until Dad suddenly picked up a letter and said, 'Gosh, this one's quite threatening – even by Willamina's standards.'

Willamina Veraminta Reginald VII Honk
Snozzle Lodge

Dear Pickled-Poops,

It is my regret to inform you that you have neglected the castle to such an extent that it is now overrun with rats. I have alerted Honkerty Council to this problem, and your entire family — including the nose-picker — are hereby summoned to attend a meeting at my house at 10 a.m. today to agree upon a pest-extermination investigation. If you do not attend, I shall tell the council you won't cooperate. The fine for vermin infestations is ₹20,000, which I'm sure is more than you paupers can afford.

Yours blah blah blah,

WH

'Rats?' Mum squawked, slamming the piano lid. 'Every castle has a few. But an infestation. I DON'T THINK SO! And how dare she call Frank a "nose-picker". And us "paupers" ... *and* the "Pickled-Poops"!'

'Save your voice, my love,' said Dad calmingly. 'We'll go round and give her a piece of our minds. It's one thing to complain about the castle's upkeep, it's quite another to insult and threaten us. And I haven't forgotten that CCTV shot of Frank and Tiffany!'

At the mention of it, Frank felt that familiar feeling of guilt bounce around his chest, which made his finger creep up his nose again.

'FRANK!' Mum trilled.

'Sorry.' *POP!* Out it came. 'Do I have to come?' he said calmly, despite his inner turmoil. 'Tiffany will be here in a minute.'

'The letter does say the "entire family",' said Dad. 'But who's she to boss us around? Just stay out of trouble – and no nose-picking in the street.'

'I promise. Anyway, me and Tiffany are going out on

a bike ride,' he lied. He felt his finger skulk towards his nostrils again, but stopped it just in time.

'The monster's here!' Frank couldn't stop himself whispering as soon as he saw Tiffany.

Tiffany almost fell off the front step. 'SOARING SLUGS!'

Frank pulled her into the hall and filled her in as quickly and as quietly as possible about:

* **the monster's arrival**
* **the slug goo drink and shower**
* **the lunchbox he'd started filling with bogeys**
* **the monster's bat friend (though unlike you, dear nose-pickers, he didn't know she was called Binky)**
* **Willamina's first letter about their nose-picking and the 'Frank monster' in her garden**
  and
* **today's second letter about the rats**

'As long as Honk-bum thinks you were in a costume and that our bogey trail was just to annoy her, I don't think we need to worry too much,' Tiffany said softly.

'I was hoping you'd say that.' Tiffany always managed to calm his nerves.

'And the rats?'

'Your guess is as good as mine.'

CHAPTER 34

BOGEY-BOGEY-BUM-BUM!

The second Mum and Dad left for Willamina's house, Frank and Tiffany dashed into the East Wing.

'I can't believe you're actually taking me to meet a real-life creature that used to be a snot tower,' Tiffany piped excitedly as they whooshed through the old dark entrance hall. There was no electricity in the East Wing, but the half-boarded windows let in enough light for them to navigate. 'I've always secretly dreamt I'd discover an unknown creature, you know.'

'Even one made of my bogeys?' asked Frank.

'Don't take all the credit, it's got my slugs' slime on it too!'

Tiffany's brown eyes widened as the monster emerged from the bat room and tottered over the potholed floor with outstretched arms.

'Goo-goo-gooey!' it said, going straight for Frank and pulling him into a long, sticky embrace.

Frank laughed, wiping gloop from his cheek. 'Monster, I think you recognize my friend Tiffany.'

For the first time in her life, Tiffany was speechless. All she could do was stare into the monster's yellow-green, bogey-rimmed eyes. Then she took a deep breath and held out her hand.

The monster immediately let go of Frank and pulled Tiffany into a bogey hug so full-on that snot stuck to her cheek.

She giggled. 'It's definitely friendly.'

Frank laughed. 'I think it likes you.'

Suddenly, four slimy things touched Tiffany's hand. It was Sammy, Violet, Peach and Slim ooching off the monster's back.

'Hey fellas!' She gave them each a tickle on their eye tentacles as they climbed up to sucker-pad themselves to her shoulder.

'We got this for you, Monster,' said Frank, holding out his old lunchbox. He and Tiffany had filled it with as many bogeys as they'd been able to muster.

The monster grabbed it thankfully and tucked in. Then it started blowing a series of raspberries, which sounded like a squidgy whoopee cushion, but actually meant, 'Follow me.'

Frank and Tiffany didn't understand, but they followed it anyway into the Werewolf Room. For a second, Tiffany stared unbelievingly at the fireplace. Then Binky swooped down to join the party with a flip and a flap, tailed by at least a thousand brown fluffy bats, sweeping around the room in an aerial ballet. Binky led them all as they swooped and looped and occasionally pooped.

At first, Frank and Tiffany dived for cover. But soon it was clear the bats were doing more than just dive-bombing and plopping. They were making shapes in the air, like clouds of starlings at sunset. And at the heart of the swirl, the bogey monster waved its webbed hands around like an orchestra conductor. There was a lightning-bolt shape here, a twisting whirlwind there . . .

'Look,' Frank cried. 'The flock looks like the monster.'

His eyebrows suddenly rose so high they almost touched his ginger curls. 'Gooliemaloolie! I think it's communicating with us! It said "gangoo" last night, but I don't think it knows any other words yet. It must be talking in shapes.'

Then the bats made a lightning-bolt shape again, which struck the mound, which morphed into a monster.

'**WAHHHHHH!**' said Frank. 'You can talk to bats and get them to do things? AND you know that you came alive because lightning struck the bogey tower?'

The monster nodded and swirled its hands to send Binky and the others back to the rafters.

'You're amazing,' said Frank.

'One of a kind,' added Tiffany.

'I think we need to find you a name.' Frank hugged the monster again. How had his bogey tower become so clever? Maybe because bogeys grow so close to your brains? 'How about Sir Greenie?'

The monster blew a disapproving raspberry.

'Or Bogey-Bogey-Bum-Bum?' Tiffany offered.

'PFFFFT!' went the monster, screwing up its face.

The friends giggled.

'Or just Bogey?' cried Frank. 'It's what you're made of.'

The monster rolled its eyeballs backwards in thought, then nodded. 'Goo-goo-gooey!' And with a big smile, it held up its webbed hand for a high five with Frank.

SQUELCH!

'Bogey it is!' Frank wiped his hand on his trousers.

CHAPTER 35

LET'S SEE WHERE THIS LEADS!

Remember that time-travelling dot?
Well it's time to press it again.

Here you go:

well done.

And this time you've travelled back **forty-two minutes** to the moment when Mum and Dad were cycling on a tandem bike down Snozzle Castle's long drive to Willamina's house and Billy and Steve were waiting in their van.

'Budge over, Steve, I can't see past your huge Scotch egg,' cried Billy, leaning into the passenger seat as Steve tucked into an early lunch.

Mum and Dad's wheels crunched past.

'Darn it, Steve, we've missed them! Why d'you always eat on the job?'

'I mon't mnow,' said Steve, spraying crumbs. He swallowed. 'Waitin' makes me hungry.'

'But we didn't see how many people were on their bikes.' Billy took a deep breath, craning his neck to see past the bushes. 'There should have been four, Steve. Two parents, the brat and his friend who got there a few minutes ago. Did you count them?'

'No. I was chewing.' Steve twiddled his pointy tash.

'For crying out loud . . .'

Billy crept up the long driveway to the front door and rang the doorbell. When no one answered, he peeked into the downstairs windows of the West Wing to double-check. Nothing. So with rucksacks bursting with everything they needed for camera-posing, the brothers set off to look for an easy way into the house.

And they found it . . .

The door to the dark and dangerous dungeon.

Billy's mouth curved into a vicious smile as the door opened with a **CREEEAK** and he peered into the chilly gloom. It gave him a thrill, as if he were back burglaring.

'Let's see where this leads.'

CHAPTER 36

UP THE CHIMNEY!

irectly above, Frank, Tiffany, Bogey, Binky and the slugs were sitting on the dusty settee in the Werewolf Room, having a jolly old time playing charades.

Their new friend was ... just ... well ... so much more than you'd expect a big booger to be.

Aside from knowing how to talk in shapes through bat choreography, he could communicate with other creatures too:

* A silverfish looking for her family
* A beetle looking for the shortest route to the garden
* Lucy Longlegs, looking for inspiration for her new song, 'I Kissed a Gargoyle and I Liked It'

As for charades, Bogey was brilliant at it because he could use Binky and the bats to make shapes for whatever he liked. So far, he had depicted:

* Sammy, Violet, Peach and Slim making slime
* a giant nose
* a finger picking that nose

and

* Binky in full flight

Bogey was just in the middle of a monumental recreation of Peach's eye tentacles when, without warning, Binky and the bats darted back to the rafters.

'Rain falling backwards?' guessed Frank.

'The bats' bedtime?' guessed Tiffany, popping Sammy, Violet, Peach and Slim back into their jar.

The monster shook his head. Ooze was suddenly

glooping down his domed forehead, like sweat, as if he could sense danger. He flattened himself against the wall, peering around the arch towards the hall.

Frank and Tiffany did the same.

Slow, heavy footsteps were sounding on its cracked marble floor.

Were Mum and Dad back? Why were they in the East Wing? But to Frank's horror, it wasn't his parents. It was . . . well, you know who, nose-pickers. It was two ornately moustachioed strangers in dark overalls (who'd traipsed through the house, from the secret cupboard to here).

Frank gasped. 'We're being burgled.'

'I don't think so,' Tiffany murmured. 'They're fixing cameras.'

Frank looked again. 'Gooliemaloolie! You're right. Who'd do a thing like that?'

But there was no time to reply, 'I HAVEN'T THE FOGGIEST!' or 'WHAT SHOULD WE DO?' or 'FOR PETE'S SAKE, CALL THE POLICE!', 'cause there, through the air, came a gruff voice saying: 'Bruv, I can hear mumbling. Over there. I thought everyone was out!' And not a second later, the men were hurling themselves towards the Werewolf Room.

'HIIIIIIDDDDDE!' yelped Frank in a whisper (something I like to call a whisp-yelp).

'GOOOOOOOOOO!' whisp-yelped Bogey.

'Up the chimney!' whisp-yelped Tiffany.

There was no time to argue.

Frank gave Bogey a leg-up into the flue, but the monster was too wide to fit and came toppling down on to Frank – **SLAM** – who toppled on to Tiffany – **BAM** – who toppled on to the floor, narrowly missing the slug jar.

This is it, thought Frank, as he lay in a sandwich of legs, soot and snot. *These men – whoever they are – are going to find us.*

NOT IF I CAN HELP IT, piped his heart as he thought of Bogey. Fighting his way to his feet, Frank braced himself for a run-in.

But then Tiffany's arms were around his ankles, and he fell again – **BAM** – banging his funny bone on a sticky-outy werewolf ear on the fireplace!

Footsteps thundered towards them.

'It's too late,' whispered Frank, stretching his tingly arm out to protect Bogey.

But the pair weren't there. In fact, no one was there.

The fireplace had revolved them into a secret room!

CHAPTER 37

STRANGE MUSEUM

The room was a small door-less study, with strange slits in the walls, like arrow loops, that let in eerie cross-shaped light. In one corner was a dusty suit of armour, set in front of a huge tapestry of zombies. In the middle was a gilded desk overlooked by an old portrait of a man dressed as a vampire hunter, wielding a cross and a wooden stake. And on the other side was a big glass case stacked with horror film posters. It was as if they'd stepped into a very small, very strange museum.

'That werewolf ear . . . WOW! It must have been the

lever that swivelled the fireplace,' said Frank, dusting off soot and a few bogeys from where his arm had scraped Bogey's leg. Bogey immediately slurped them back up.

The friends stood there trembling, taking it all in.

'This must be the secret study of Dad's superfan – you know, Henri Conk. Look, there's even a framed poster from Dad's most famous film, *Revenge of the Saber-toothed Ape*,' Frank whispered.

Then, from somewhere through the wall of their new hiding place, they heard the men:

'Gawd. I was sure there were voices in here!'

'Maybe the place is haunted?'

'Doubt it, bruv. But it *is* strange. Let's just put this last camera up and get out. We'll turn 'em on when we're back at ICU HQ. Not a word of this to anyone, all right?'

'All right.'

Then it went quiet.

'Who on earth would want to spy on you?' said Tiffany. 'And what's ICU HQ?'

'I don't know, but it can't be good.' Frank tried to appear

calm, but inside he was mushier than a squidgepea (which, nose-pickers, is a squashy booger shaped like a pea).

Bogey didn't look good either. Real squidgepeas were pearling on his bumpy forehead, which meant that he was very frightened, which meant that those men had to be very nasty. He was too good at sensing things in animals to get it wrong in humans.

'We should tell your parents,' said Tiffany.

'NO!' Frank cried. He knew that he *should* tell them, but another worry was nibbling his nose hair and he couldn't ignore it: 'They'll find out about Bogey.' *And stop loving me,* he added silently. 'First, we need to find out more. And until we do, we keep this to ourselves and Bogey stays hidden, OK?'

'But we can't just leave the cameras in place for those men to spy on us,' cried Tiffany.

Frank frowned.

'No, we can't,' he said. 'So, let's do something about it – before they're switched on.'

CHAPTER 38

TAKE COOOOOOOVVVVVVEEEEEEER!!!!!!!!

Frank gazed around the study and jumped on the spot to think. 'There must be something in here we can use.'

There was loads of cool stuff . . .

* a sparkly green brooch shaped like an axe in the desk drawer

* a book of spooky drawings and symbols on the mantelpiece

and

* a box marked 'to fend off the Vampyre' containing

the same cross and wooden stake depicted in the painting

. . . but nothing they could use on the cameras.

Until . . .

Frank pulled back the zombie tapestry.

'What about this?' he cried. It was an antique slingshot mounted on a rusty hook.

'Woah!' said Tiffany. 'Your house is officially the best place ever!'

Frank inspected the slingshot. It was old and dusty, but the leather still had stretch in it. 'We could fire rocks at them!'

'But we haven't got any,' Tiffany observed.

'Oh yeah!' Frank scratched his ginger head.

'GOO!' said Bogey excitedly, pointing to his own bogey-rimmed hooter.

'Of course!' Frank cried. He still couldn't get over how clever Bogey was. 'We could fire snot to cover the lenses. Dad always says specks of dust can ruin images – imagine a whole splat of gloop!'

And so, dear nose-pickers, prepare yourselves (I recommend you wear a plastic mac). This next bit's called **OPERATION SLING-SNOT.** It takes place all over the Wing, on the other side of that revolving fireplace, and it was their stickiest, snottiest mission yet.

Ready? TAKE **COOOOOOOVVVVVVEEEEEEER!!!!!!!!**

CHAPTER 39

OPERATION SLING-SNOT

SPLATCH! SPLATCH!

'Twas a fast and sticky storm of gluey, sloppy snot that Frank and Tiffany took turns at sling-shooting through the air to coat every camera they could find.

SPLATCH! SPLATCH! SPLATCH!

And when the children's nostrils could provide no more, Bogey scraped some greenies from in between his webbed toes and flung them at the cameras too.

SPLATCH! SPLATCH! SPLATCH!

AND THEN, when no amount of sneezing could replenish Frank and Tiffany's supplies, and Bogey had donated as much of himself as he could safely part with, Binky and the bats saved the day by pooping on the cameras. It was teamwork at its gooiest and pooiest, and within twenty minutes, the friends felt sure that they'd smothered every camera in the East Wing.

And it was a good thing too, 'cause:

BEEEEEEEEEEEEEEEEP!

'The cameras are switching on,' shrieked Tiffany.

Bogey immediately shot off back through the fireplace, clutching the slug jar, followed by the bats.

'Stay hidden,' shouted Frank.

Frank and Tiffany ran towards the door to the West Wing.

'I hope we've done the right thing!' said Tiffany, dashing through.

'Me too,' Frank hollered, locking the door behind them.

One second later, Mum and Dad got back (all pink-cheeked from the tandem ride they'd taken to clear their heads after their meeting).

All they saw were Frank and Tiffany sprinting down the corridor.

But someone else had seen more, **MUCH MORE**.

CHAPTER 40

TOP-SECRET PLAN

S tanding in the I—

STOP!

Sorry!

Look at me, getting ahead of myself.

I almost told you **WHO** had seen more, **MUCH MORE,** but I can't do that yet 'cause there's something important you need to know first: how things had gone at Willamina's house not an hour earlier.

And so the answer is:

Very badly for Mr and Mrs Pickerty-Boop, who hadn't

managed to get a word in edgeways, but **WONDERFULLY** for Willamina, who (once the Pickerty-Boops had assured her that Frank wasn't there because he and Tiffany had gone out on their bikes) had felt as chirpy as a chaffinch, convinced that the Bashers would now be fitting the cameras and that things in general were finally going her way.

You see, this whole rat nonsense hadn't just been a ruse to get the family out of the house for the camera-fitting. Oh no (though it had worked very well for that). It was actually now the very thing that would allow her to take the castle!

WHAT?

HOW?

I KNOW!

Remember back in Chapter 30 when I said Willamina had finally found the thing she'd been looking for in documents she'd stolen from Honkerty Library? Well, that thing wasn't just the plan of Snozzle for the Bashers, it was also . . .

A 50 per cent off voucher for polka-dot dental braces?

An old sausage roll with rare black mould?

A piece of chewed gum from the 1950s?

Nah! 'Twas the deeds to Snozzle Castle! Which – as you will know – means the castle contract between her eccentric uncle, Henri Conk, and Frank's dad! It was a whole page long and it contained something very useful. It read:

Henri Conk's Gift to Stanley Pickerty-Boop

I, Henri Conk, grant you, Stanley Pickerty-Boop, Snozzle Castle on condition that it never gets infested with vermin. All castles have a few uninvited visitors, but only those left to rot and crumble get properly overrun.

SO in a nutshell, Stanley: if the castle gets choked with vermin, it means you're not looking after the place and it will revert back to me, if I'm alive, or my next in line if I'm not.

There!

Now enjoy the property. It's somewhat tumbledown, but nothing you, oh wondrous film director, won't be able to handle.

Henri Conk

PS *Don't fall in the moat. A big eel lives there ~ apparently.*

'Choked with vermin!' Willamina had laughed. 'Then the place reverts back to your next in line. Oh Henri, you ridiculous, childless man. That's me - your niece. Oh joy!'

And now, what luck! Not only did she have a pair of ICU men who could pose the cameras, but she also had a pair who could catch the vermin - rats, she'd decided. They were nasty little biters and meaner than other pests.

Oooh, how she'd laugh when the CCTV showed not only what the family was up to, but also their faces when they saw the rats. Then she'd screenshot the scene and get all the proof she needed!

But how would she get the rats inside the castle?

Ah. That was PART 2 of her top-secret plan: all she had to do was worry the Pickerty-Boops so much that they'd call the pest exterminators (who were really the ICU men). Then the brothers would go back to Snozzle Castle to lay boxfuls of traps. Except – and this was the REALLY clever part – the boxes wouldn't contain traps, they'd contain vermin! The very stinking, seething ratty-ratty-rat-rats that she needed to break the contract.

Oh, how cunning she'd been! How clever!

Once the rats had taken root, Snozzle Castle, her rightful inheritance, would be hers.

For ever!

The End

Not really – just the end of the first thing I needed to tell you.

CHAPTER 41

WHO'D SEEN MORE, MUCH MORE!

So here's the second:

It was Willamina Honk who'd seen more, **MUCH MORE** - which I bet you'd already guessed, you clever nosey-wosey picky-wickies!

Though to find out what she'd seen, we'll have to jump forwards in time (with a silly word, remember) to the moment after the cameras had switched on.

Shout:

LOLLYGAG!

(Which you'd think'd mean 'choking on your ice lol', but it doesn't. It means 'messing around' – which is something I bet you nose-pickers do a lot!)

Oh look. It's worked!

Standing in the ICU HQ office with the Bashers, Willamina stopped dead in her high heels: a grey haze was blocking half the cameras and she'd just seen the boy. TWICE!!!!!! Once running down the corridor with his friend in the West Wing; and AGAIN in the East Wing, going through a fireplace in the swamp monster costume!

(For yes, alas, nose-pickers, unbeknown to the snot-slinging friends, they'd missed a camera! **A VERY IMPORTANT CAMERA**. The **VERY** camera that was trained on the werewolf fireplace! And now Bogey had been spotted!)

'Impossible,' squeaked Willamina, blinking hard. 'No one can be in two places at once!' Then that unsettling feeling she'd had in her garden came rushing back. That hideous lolloping tongue! The weird way it had stood with all those animals. The foul way its green, pustule-ridden face had melted when she'd hosed it. It had to have been the boy in a costume. And yet . . .

'Did you see that?' she whispered to Billy, a bubble of realization fizzing down her silk-stockinged legs into her strangely hairy bunions (she'd tried shaving but it always grew back thicker).

'Yeah! But I wouldn't worry,' he said, distracted by the blurry screens. It looked like something was stuck on the cameras, which was very annoying. 'It's probably just some sort of funny vermin. They come in all shapes and sizes.' (He'd seen his fair share of oddities over the years – a three-tailed beaver, a seven-pawed mouse, even a two-headed ferret dragging a brolly and a mobile phone.) He bet that was what they'd heard in the Werewolf Room.

'You *pantalon de cuir*. Rats are vermin. This is a . . . a . . .' She didn't know what it was. But it was a monstrosity, all right. And it was clearly contaminating her beloved castle! HOW DARE that hideous family breed it there. HOW DARE they use it to humiliate her. What sort of dangerous weirdos was she dealing with?

There was only one thing to do.

'POP ITS CLOGS!' she screeched, then sneezed (blast her wretched cold). 'Here's what's going to happen. I'll stay here to watch the screens while you two wait for the family to call. Once you've released the rats as we discussed, I want you to go through that fireplace and find the abomination. But don't kill it . . . YET! I want you to bring it back here where I can watch you do it and make sure it's truly dead.' She didn't want to risk it – whatever it was – not dying and getting back into the castle once she had the keys! 'Got it?'

'Got it,' Billy cried, thinking her battier than ever. 'But killin' isn't in our contract, so we'll want extra,' he added, seeing an opportunity.

'Extra? Well, I was about to dock seventy thousand from your salary for those blurry screens. I want to see the family everywhere, remember, and get evidence!' The fireplace angle would be enough to screenshot her rat proof, but the brothers didn't need to know that! 'But how about I add it back on, and we call it even?'

'Wha—?!' Billy gritted his teeth. He'd not seen that one coming. She'd beaten him at his own money game.

'Something wrong?' Willamina smiled sweetly.

'No,' Billy murmured, his moustache suddenly ruffled.

BINGO! thought Willamina. She had always enjoyed watching lowly employees squirm. 'Now **CHOP CHOP**. Back to work!'

CHAPTER 41¾

LAST WARNING!

And so, nose-pickers, now would be a good time for a cup of tea, a quick wee, or even another one of those Bally-Wally Balls. Whatever makes you feel good. Because I told you things were about to get worse, much worse, and it's from here onwards that it happens.

This is your LAST WARNING! Good luck!

PS If you've run out of Bally-Wallys, I'll give you my recipe for them if you promise to shout

BOGEY BOOGIE WOOGIE

ten times in the playground next time you're at school!
You will?

Great! Then, here you go:

❋ **2 bananas**
❋ **300g of white chocolate**
❋ **green food colouring**
❋ **10 lollipop sticks**

Cut the bananas into ten pieces. Shove a lolly stick in each piece. Melt the chocolate (with help from a grown-up, please – though don't show them the rest of this book, remember). Mix in green food colouring (carefully, it can get everywhere; I found some in my ear last week). Dip the banana chunks in the chocolate. Let them cool. Scoff. **Nice one.**

CHAPTER 42

I DON'T KNOW WHAT TO DO!

Over at Snozzle Castle, Frank's dad had called an emergency meeting around the kitchen table.

'Kids, have you seen any rats in this house?' he said.

'No,' Frank and Tiffany chorused.

'Are you sure?' He was stirring his cuppa so fast the tea turned into a whirlpool.

'Of course they haven't,' snapped Mum, ''cause there aren't any! How dare that old battleaxe humiliate us like that.' She stuffed leftover custard into her mouth.

'She is a battleaxe,' said Dad. 'But, right now, we can't afford a big fine, so even if Honk's making this up, we still need to call the pest exterminators, to make doubly sure.'

Dad whipped out a business card from his trouser pocket and dialled the number with his mobile phone.

As Dad spoke, Frank and Tiffany leant over to look at the card. Their eyes popped out of their sockets – not really (that would have been messy), but nearly. There, as plain as day, were the initials ICU!

'Where did he get that from?' Frank asked Mum.

'On the floor by the letter box,' she said. 'Good timing, really.'

'This can't be a coincidence,' whispered Tiffany. 'I've got the willy-willy-woo-woos. You should tell your Mum and Dad now.'

'NO!' said Frank, a little too loudly. He had the willy-willy-woo-woos too, but he didn't think he could tell Mum and Dad about any of this without mentioning Bogey.

'What are you two disagreeing about?' said Mum.

'Um . . . nothing,' Frank said, fake-smiling. But Tiffany

had a point. Perhaps he should say something? Not a lot. Just enough to stop his parents from letting the men into the house. 'Um . . . I don't think you should trust the ICU people,' he blurted.

'Why ever not?' said Mum.

'I . . . er . . . don't like their name,' he improvised. 'They sound dodgy.'

'Don't be silly,' said Mum. 'I-C-U sounds like they really care!'

'Right!' Dad spun round and put his phone away. 'They said they'd be here in a few minutes, so I s'pose the first thing we should do is check the East Wing.'

'The East Wing?' Frank almost choked. Things were going from bad to worse!

'Yes. We've not seen any rats in this side of the house, but we haven't been in the East Wing for what . . . two years?'

'Easily,' said Mum.

'If we can't find any vermin there, then the pest exterminators won't either.'

'Well, we'll HELP!' Frank suddenly blurted, 'cause for a silly second, he thought that somehow, by offering his and Tiffany's services, he'd manage to find a way to stop his parents from going in.

He could pretend to faint?

Or tell them he'd seen rats outside?

Or rush into the East Wing and lock them out . . . and get Tiffany to refuse to open the door?

Oh **Gooliemaloolie**, *no. None of that'll work.*

'I *suppose* you can come. Just this once,' agreed Mum. 'But the floor's very holey and dangerous and I don't want you looking for rats by yourselves, all right?'

'Yes,' said Frank, but this was not all right. **NOT. ALL. RIGHT. AT. ALL!**

'I don't know what to do,' he whispered to Tiffany.

'Nor do I, but Bogey's hidden for now, so let's just go with the flow.'

Frank nodded. Tiffany always gave sound advice. He just hoped Bogey would stay hidden – and that his parents wouldn't die of shock when they saw the sticky state of the East Wing.

CHAPTER 43

BAAAAAAAAAAAAAAAA TTTTTTTTTTTTTTSSS SSSSSSS!

They didn't die. But they were shocked. And as the dung-tinged bogey breeze of the East Wing nipped their nostrils, Frank's parents cried, 'URGH! URGH! URGH!' followed by a long list of naughty words I can only mention if you make me a triple-layer cheddar sandwich with mayo, gherkins and lettuce, **NOW**.

What? You haven't got any cheese?

Well, sorry. Maybe next time.

'How did it get in this state?' Mum gulped. She was almost as green as the sling-snot.

'Maybe we do have an infestation after all,' said Dad, looking around the hall. He wasn't green, he was grey.

'What are you going to do?' Frank asked, his voice suddenly squeaky. Maybe if he could find out his parents' intentions, he could think up a plan.

'Start cleaning up,' said Dad. 'There's clearly something unusual going on here. And look, some of this poo's green. Goodness knows what the rats have been eating.'

Frank turned away to hide his finger skulking up his nose. Then he looked up to check the cameras. They were still invisible under the pooey-bogey sludge, which was a small relief at least.

'Now come *ooooooooon.*' Mum ushered Frank and Tiffany towards the door in a low F. 'I want you both in the West Wing. It's too disgusting here. What would your parents think, Tiffany? I'm going to start scrubbing before the pest people arrive. I don't want them seeing this – it's embarrassing. And I'm starting in this hall, in three seconds. So, off you *go-o-o-o-o-o-o-o-o-o-o-o!*'

'You know what this means don't you?' said Frank, closing the bedroom door firmly behind them. 'Everyone who shouldn't be in the East Wing is in there, or will be any second now, and we're stuck in here, without a plan!'

'We need to warn Bogey. And the bats. And the slugs,' added Tiffany with a quiver in her voice.

'But we can't get into the secret room without going through the fireplace. Mum or Dad might see us. Or the ICU men might, once they get here again. Do you think it's Honk-bum who sent them? She's the one who posted the rat letter. She could have dropped the ICU card through too. Though I can't think why she'd do all this – unless!' He gasped. 'It *does* have something to do with Bogey? What if she's somehow realized it wasn't me in the garden? Gooliemaloolie, we need to get to him!' Frank jumped on the spot for a second, before flopping on to the floor, crying, 'But it's impossible.'

'Not if . . .' shouted Tiffany, with a smile creeping up

her face.

'Yes?' said Frank.

'Not if we take the secret tunnel to get out of the house, then go through the garden to slip through the Werewolf Room window. If we're careful, we can get between the window and the fireplace without being seen. Then we can be with Bogey and listen out for the men together. I don't see how anyone could know about the secret room.'

Not five minutes later, the friends landed with a soft thud on the floor below the roosting bats.

Frank flattened his back against the wall and peered towards the scratch-scratch of scrubbing in the hall. Mum's and Dad's backs were turned. 'Now,' he whispered.

One step.

He and Tiffany rushed to the dusty settee and ducked down behind it.

Two steps.

They dashed towards the fireplace.

Three steps.

Surprised by the children's sudden appearance, Binky and the bats rushed down to greet them with very loud **EEKs**.

'OH NO!'

Mum whisked round.

'BAAAAAAAAAAAAAATTTTTTTTTTTTTTSSSSSSSSSS!'

she screamed in an ear-piercing G (which cracked an old mirror).

'QUIIIIIIIIICCCCCCK!'

yelped Frank, pulling the werewolf ear.

Frank's parents saw nothing but bats retreating up the flue.

But Willamina had seen more, **MUCH MORE – AGAIN!**

CHAPTER 44

SAY WAKEY WAKEY

'Leave all the talkin' to me, bruv,' said Billy, pressing the doorbell of Snozzle Castle. They'd successfully tranquillized all seventy-three of the furry squirmers and safely packed them into the traps, which they'd brought with them on a trolley.

Billy looked at his phone clock impatiently and pressed the bell again.

'Come on!' He was raring to get everything over and done with so they could get their big fat cheque and go!

Mr and Mrs Pickerty-Boop finally appeared, dripping

in bat poo and (unbeknown to them) Frank and Tiffany's snot.

'I'm so sorry for our appearance AND the smell,' said Mum. 'We've had a little . . . hiccup.'

'I can see that,' said Billy, pushing past rudely.

Steve came up the rear with the traps and mumbled an offhand, 'Hello.'

'We'll start in the East Wing,' said Billy, wanting to see what was on the cameras.

'Good,' said Dad, ruefully opening the East Wing door. "Cause . . . well, see for yourselves . . .'

The whiff knocked everyone for six.

Billy had rarely seen a place so revolting, which was saying something.

'We think it's guano,' said Mum (which is posh for bat poo). 'You see, I don't think we have rats. We have ba—'

'We'll be the judge of that,' said Billy, cutting her off nastily and looking up. But she was right. Guano was all over the cameras. And some of it was green! URGH! How had bats made the East Wing such a poo-fest so fast? Billy glared. If it hadn't been for that gunk, they'd have wangled more money out of the Honkster!

He hustled the Pickerty-Boops into a corner where they couldn't see what was going on. 'Stay here,' he ordered so firmly that all they could do was say, 'Yes . . . OK.'

'Shout if you need us,' Dad called after him, trying to sound as if he were still in control. Then he hugged Mum tight. So much hung on the success of this visit. *They couldn't afford a £20,000 fine from Honkerty Council.*

The brothers squelched through the East Wing as if they owned the joint, ignoring the stench and gloop, and dropping rat boxes every few metres.

'We'll release 'em in here,' Billy said, stepping into the Werewolf Room. Then he smoothed his ruffled moustache and extracted a control device from his bag. 'Right. Time to release the rats. Say "wakey wakey", Steve.'

'WAKEY WAKEY, STEVE!' said Steve, brandishing a rat taser in case the nippers got nippy.

Billy pushed a button that opened the traps and gave the sleeping rats an electric shock. **CRRRZZZZZZZ!**

The critters sprang from their cages, hissing angrily, then scampered across the floor.

'OH DEAR!' shouted Billy to Frank's parents across the wing. 'You've got bats AND rats. Look. We've found a rat nest.'

'It's not possible,' cried Frank's dad, even as four rats ran across his feet. He and Mum strode over. 'Where?'

'Here,' Billy lied, pointing under the dusty settee.

'Thank goodness you brought traps. Are you sure they'll work?' said Dad, his voice as shaky as his innards.

'Very sure,' said Billy.

'And what about the bats?'

'We'll deal with them in time.'

'Thank you,' said Mum. 'Gosh, I need a cuppa.'

DRIIIING!!!!!

It was Billy's phone. He strolled out of earshot, then a minute later was back with his best fake smile. 'Did I hear you mention tea?'

'Er, yes,' said Mum. 'Would you like one?'

'We'd love one,' said Billy.

'Got any Tomlinson's Extra Dark chocolate?' Steve butted in.

'Isn't that made with mouse droppings?' said Dad.

'I think so.' Steve smiled.

'Just get them what they want,' whispered Mum. 'We need a good report.'

'Right. I'll pop to the shops,' said Dad, bemused.

And at that, he and Mum squelched out of the East Wing.

'Right, Steve,' said Billy, checking they were alone. 'That was Honk. She says the kids are with the vermin behind that revolving fireplace! And we're to go through now, while the parents are gone. Get the body bag ready!'

CHAPTER 45

TRAPPED!

Frank couldn't believe his eyes, but suddenly there they were! Rats – dozens of them – pouring in through the fireplace to line up like little soldiers on the floor as Bogey, with Binky on his shoulder, gurgled things only the animals could understand.

'How on earth did these fellas get into the castle?' Frank said.

Bogey growled gently at a big brown rat at the front, then replied **'GI-GEE-GU!'**

'We should have guessed!' Frank gasped.

Tiffany pressed her ear to the fireplace, trying to hear what was going on. 'Oh, no. I think your mum and dad have just left, Frank,' she whispered. 'But I can still hear the ICU men.'

'What are they saying?'

There was no time to answer.

A grating noise sounded and the fireplace floor began to move.

The rats scarpered in all directions.

Tiffany had to roll off the revolving floor to stay in the room.

'Bogey, hide,' Frank whisp-yelped.

Bogey rushed behind the zombie tapestry. But it wasn't a very good hiding place. His body looked like a big bump in the wall and his webbed toes poked out the bottom.

Frank and Tiffany ran in front of him for extra concealment, but both knew the obvious: they were well and truly

TRAPPED!

CHAPTER 46

ONE. TWO. THR—!

'**W**ell, well, well,' cried Billy as he and Steve emerged from the hearth like huge, ornately moustachioed brick walls, with evil grins on their faces.

Then what happened next happened so swiftly, I'll have to use slow motion to show you.

SSSEEENNNSSSIIINNNGG IIIMMMIIINNNEEE- NNNTTT DDDAAANNNGGGEEERRR, BBBOOOGGGEEEYYY GGGOOOTTT

BBBIIINNNKKKYYY AAANNNDDD HHHEEERRR BBBAAATTT FFFRRRIIIEEENNNDDDS TTTOO AAATTTTTTAAACCCKKK...

Sorry, slow motion's hard. You'll have to imagine the next bit's slow.

Sensing imminent danger, Bogey got Binky and her bat friends to attack the intruders, slapping and poo-bombing as much as they could. But Steve had his rat taser out!

'Take that!' he cried. **CRZZZZZZZZZZZZZ!!!!!**

The bats dropped to the floor like winged ragdolls.

'Who's next?' shouted Billy with a nasty glint in his eye.

A group of rats leapt at them, but in seconds they'd suffered the same fate.

Frank stood his ground, trying not to look at the piles of animal bodies in case he blubbed. 'Stay back!' he shouted. The rest of the rats hid.

'Oooh,' said Billy mockingly. 'You're scary... NOT. Hand it over.'

'Hand what over?' said Frank.

'The verminy thing behind the tapestry. I can see its feet,' Billy sneered. 'Just shove it in here and we'll be gone.'

Steve gave the black plastic body bag a menacing jiggle.

'I can't see anything,' said Frank, moving to the opposite end of the tapestry and pulling it back to reveal the stone wall. 'You must be seeing things.' He was surprised at how brave that sounded. He'd never been so scared in his life.

Tiffany's eyes darted nervously between the men and the desk as she realized that she'd left the slug jar in full sight. Sammy, Violet, Peach and Slim were inside, cowering behind a lettuce leaf.

Billy noticed too. 'And what's this?' he said, grabbing the jar.

'Put them down!' shouted Tiffany.

'Oh, they're your friends, are they?' Billy said in a mocking voice.

'No, it's just ...' She tried to think of an excuse. 'They're poisonous, and I wouldn't like you to fall ill,' she lied.

Billy and Steve looked at her for a moment then burst out laughing. They'd always enjoyed being mean to kids.

'Tell you what. Bring me that thing and we won't taser

your slugs.'

Frank was horror-struck, but tried to contain himself.
'I told you, there's nothing there.'

'Oh, but we all know there is,' said Billy.

Steve raised the taser and made blue electricity zigzag into the air.

The slugs quaked together in a heap, their eye tentacles sucked into their bodies to make themselves as small as possible.

Billy prodded Binky with his shoe. 'The bats and rats will probably wake up in half an hour . . . probably. But a tasered slug? It'll turn to slop. Just give it over. It's the only way to save your slimers.'

Steve frazzled the air again, moving the stun gun ever closer to the lip of the jar. **CRZZZZZZZZZZZ!**

'NOOOOOOOOOOOOOOO!' screamed Tiffany.

'MEEP, MEEP, MEEEEEEEEP!' screamed the slugs, which meant, 'Tell our mums we love *theeeeeemmmmm.*'

Steve laughed. He was enjoying the action.

'You've got 'til three,' Billy said. **'ONE . . .TWO . . .THR—!'**

'GAAAAAAA!'

CHAPTER 47

GOO-GOO-GO!

t was Bogey as he stepped out from behind the tapestry. He growled it again for good measure: **'GAAAAAAAA!'**

'Gawd!' cried Billy. 'What sort of vermin is it?' He'd never seen anything quite like THAT! It made him want to retch, so he did.

Twice!

'REEETCH! REEETCH!'

Then he gathered his thoughts. Who cared what it was when it was the key to their pay cheque.

'Steve, pass me the bag,' he said calmly, keeping the slug

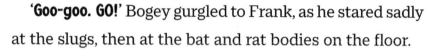

jar in one hand (and trying not to look at the creature).

Steve kept the taser crackling.

'**Goo-goo. GO!**' Bogey gurgled to Frank, as he stared sadly at the slugs, then at the bat and rat bodies on the floor.

Frank was quite struck by the last word. It was a definitely a 'go' and not a 'goo'. And he knew exactly what it meant. Bogey had seen enough injured friends for one day. He was going to sacrifice himself for the slugs and GO with the ICU men.

'**Don't do it,**' Frank cried.

But Bogey just looked at Frank with love in his bright yellow-green eyes (and squidgepeas on his brow) and stepped towards Billy.

'That's right, this way,' Billy coaxed nastily, wiggling the bag. '**REEETCH!**' Gawd, he couldn't stop himself.

'Get away from him,' cried Frank, charging at Billy and kicking his shins.

Tiffany joined in too, stamping on Billy's toes and making a grab for the slug jar. She missed, so she pulled his long moustache.

Steve yanked the friends off his brother, tossing them across the room like cockroaches. They slammed into the desk – which hurt A LOT.

'Nobody touches the moustache!' cried Billy, smoothing his furry appendage. 'You'll get the slugs if and when that thing goes with us.' He turned to Bogey. 'So, get in the bag! **REEEETCH!**'

Bogey indicated to Billy to put the bag down so that he could step into it.

Frank made a dive for the suit of armour by the tapestry and hurled a boot at Billy.

But Steve caught it mid-air.

'Nice try,' mocked Billy. 'Now say cheerio to your friend. And don't try to follow or the slugs are a goner.'

'MEEEEEEEP!!!'

'Why are you doing this?' cried Frank.

'None of your business!' shouted Billy.

Frank suddenly found himself blubbing. How could he have let this happen? There was Bogey, up to his waist in plastic, probably about to come to a sticky end and he couldn't do a thing about it.

'I'm sorry,' he whimpered.

Bogey just smiled and looked Frank straight in the eyes. **'Gangoo,'** he said as Billy pulled the body bag up around his head.

'Can I taser him for the journey?' asked Steve, crackling the air.

'Course you can,' said Billy.

And before you could say *frazzle my freckles*, Steve had zapped Bogey - **CRZZZZZZZZZZ** - and Billy had smashed the slug jar in spite!

Then the ICU men were away through the fireplace.

CHAPTER 48

FOLLOW THAT VAN!

'**S**TOP THEM!**'** cried Frank and Tiffany, bursting into the West Wing seconds later.

Through the window, Frank could just make out the men throwing Bogey into the back of their van and whooshing off down the driveway with a screech of tyres.

'What are you doing here?' cried Mum, arriving with two mugs of tea.

'We thought you were in your room,' said Dad, holding Steve's chocolate bar. 'Those men are very efficient.'

In a split second, Frank decided to do something Tiffany

had told him to do earlier: tell Mum and Dad. They might not want anything more to do with him afterwards, but it was the least he could do – for Bogey. He just didn't think he and Tiffany could save their friend alone.

'Mum, Dad, I've something to confess,' he cried. 'I know it's bad, but I built a bogey tower. It got struck by lightning during the storm, and now it's turned into a monster called Bogey. But he's really kind. And clever. And talks to bats and other animals. We hid him in a secret room in the East Wing. I know I wasn't supposed to be there. But the ICU men have just tasered him and bogeynapped him. They put cameras in the East Wing, and we think they brought the rats too, and that Willamina Honk's behind it all – though we don't know why. And Bogey might be dead – or he might die soon! So we've got to save him! Will you help?'

There was a heavy silence. Then . . .

Mum burst out laughing so hard she blew a raspberry! **'PFFFFFFT!'**

'Don't fib,' said Dad, swallowing a giggle. **'HA HA**

HAAAAAAAA!' And then he couldn't stop. 'Frank, that's one of the best stories I've ever heard. **HA HA HAAAAAAAA!** I couldn't have put that in a film if I'd tried. In fact, maybe I should.' He reached into his pocket for his Idea Notebook.

'But it's true,' Tiffany protested. 'Look, they're getting away.'

Dad turned to the window and saw the ICU van now at the end of the drive. 'They probably – **HA HA HA** – just had another urgent call.'

'But they smashed my slug jar.' She parted her hair to reveal Sammy, Violet, Peach and Slim hiding among the curls.

Mum and Dad roared even more.

'I'm sorry, Tiffany, but that's fantastic!' cried Dad. 'How ever did you get them to do that? Hold still, while I get my phone out!'

'Forget it! Let's go,' cried Frank, pulling Tiffany (slugs 'n' all) towards the front door. 'We need to save Bogey. NOW! We need to follow that van!'

CHAPTER 49

DON'T EVER DO THIS AT HOME!

They jumped on Tiffany's bike, with Tiffany pedalling furiously and Frank on the seat behind.

Off they sped beyond the gates of Snozzle Castle. Down they turned into Sneaky Beak Lane.

Left they whooshed out of Snout Back Alley – all the time searching for the ICU van.

'I can't see it anywhere,' said Tiffany, taking one hand off the handlebars to check the slugs were still there. They were.

'Try Honkerty-Honk-Honk,' said Frank (which was the

village's silly name for the main road).

Off they zoomed towards it but . . .

'AHHHHHHHH!'

. . . they rolled straight towards Bo Jacobs and Squishy the hamster, who was performing an intricate ballroom dancing number.

Squishy's cage went flying. Bo did too.

'Sorry!' they shouted. But they couldn't stop, for there, finally, driving off at full speed from the next set of traffic lights along the main road, was the van!

'We need to go faster,' cried Frank.

'My legs feel like fire. Swap with me,' puffed Tiffany.

The friends switched, then flew off again. But by now the traffic lights had changed to RED!

'We've got to stop,' Frank cried.

'Keep pedalling,' squealed Tiffany.

'I can't. There are cars coming.'

'JUST KEEP GOING!!!!!'

'MEEEEP!' went the slugs.

Nose-pickers, don't ever do this at home!

Frank closed his eyes and jumped the lights, powering forward in a straight line, praying nothing would hit them. He heard Tiffany cry out in terror as Walter Wills the grocer's car whooshed towards them.

Walter slammed on the brakes.

The car skidded towards the bike.

Walter turned the wheel round hard to avoid them and . . . hit a tree. 'You—' The rest of his words disappeared behind a big **BEEEEEP** (thank goodness; they were incredibly rude) as he honked his horn and an entire pack of sprouts flew up into the air to land SPLAT on his head.

But onwards rode the friends, trying not to think of the chaos they'd caused. Onwards behind the van. Onwards to the . . .

'ICU HQ!' panted Frank, reading the sign on a low-rise building, fronted with battered garage doors where the words 'Car Repair Shop' had been crossed out. 'We should have guessed!'

They hid behind some bins across the street and watched the ICU van stop not by the garage door, but around the side where a big water tank was hooked to a trailer. The nasty pair opened the van to grab Bogey, still lifeless in the bag. Then Billy flung him roughly over his shoulder like a pile of rubbish and, checking the coast was clear, took out a key and entered the building through a side door.

'**GOOLIEMALOOLIE!** We need to act now,' cried Frank.

Without thinking of his own safety, he shot off after the men towards the side door, but the pavement was uneven and – **SMACK!** – he tripped over a raised stone and ran straight into the door.

Miracle one: His foot struck the door the instant before it should have closed.

Miracle two: The men had already disappeared through a second door at the end of the corridor and didn't notice a thing.

Tiffany ran up to Frank. 'You OK?' she whispered, helping him to his feet.

'Yes.' Frank smiled. 'Look. We're in!'

CHAPTER 50

FIRE ARMS!

The friends skulked cautiously along the brightly lit corridor, their eyes and ears straining for signs of the ICU men. They slowly pushed open the second door and found themselves in a small, grey warehouse, with old oil stains on the floor, and floor-to-ceiling shelves filled with all sorts of dodgy stuff: axes, crowbars, metal cages, boxed CCTV cameras like the ones fitted in the castle, electric wires, electronic circuit boards, hoses and ropes of various thickness and – **GOOLIEMALOOLIE** – a crate marked 'fire arms'! Not gun firearms, but shop mannequin arms saved from a fire! And they were all blackened and half melted and poking out the top like something from one of Dad's horror films.

'I don't like this,' whispered Tiffany. 'Where do you think the men have gone?'

It was eerily silent.

'The door over there says "office" on it,' whispered Frank.

Filled with foreboding, they moved quietly towards it, checking left and right for any sign of movement.

'Here goes,' said Frank, pushing the door and bracing himself for a run-in with the enemy. But the ICU men weren't there!

Frank and Tiffany sighed with relief.

It was short-lived.

For there on the wall were not posters about the latest camera technology or nice, smiley photos of happy former customers like you'd expect in a normal CCTV company office. No. Every inch of the wall was covered in screens, and all of them showed somewhere in – you guessed it –

Frank's home!

Frank couldn't believe it. There were Mum and Dad, no longer laughing, and drinking tea in the kitchen, clear as day. And the moment he saw it, he felt silly because, *Doh! Of course the ICU men put cameras in the West Wing.* With his parents out, why would they have limited themselves to just the abandoned parts? As Mum put her head in her hands, a swirl of guilt twisted in his stomach. But there was no time to dither.

'Look!' Tiffany gasped. There was also an old plan of Snozzle Castle on the wall, marked with dots showing everywhere the men had fitted the cameras. And next to it, on a little table, was a blue file with a document that said, 'Deeds to Snozzle Castle'. Frank opened it and saw a page entitled 'Henri Conk's Gift to Stanley Pickerty-Boop'. One paragraph was neatly underlined in red:

If the castle gets choked with vermin, it means you're not looking after the place and it will revert back to me, if I'm alive, or my next in line if I'm not.

'The rats!' said Frank. 'That's what all this is about: stealing Snozzle. It looks like Henri Conk's letter to my dad, giving him the castle.'

'And here's who wants the castle,' whispered Tiffany, holding another page covered in neat handwriting:

I, Willamina Veraminta Reginald VII Conk, do solemnly swear that I am Henri Conk's next in line and as such – with the clear evidence that Snozzle Castle has been ruined by the Pickerty-Boop family and is overrun with vermin – I hereby take ownership of said castle. So there!

'We thought she was involved, but **"CONK"? CONK?** Her real name's **CONK?** She changed it to **HONK**, but it's **CONK! CONK! CONK!**' It wasn't a rap. It was Frank feeling sick and angry.

But - nose-pickers - there was **STILL WORSE TO COME!** And I'll call it **Exhibits A** and **B**:

Exhibit A: In the file was a printed-out screenshot of

rats scampering in the Werewolf Room, with the word 'PROOF!' scribbled in red ink.

Exhibit B: Below it was a shot of Bogey going through the fireplace, with the words, **'ABOMINATION BRED IN MY PROPERTY. IT. MUST. DIE!'**

Frank gasped. They'd missed a camera! That's how the ICU men and Willamina had found out about Bogey. That's why Bogey's life was in danger. Of all the cameras to . . . ! He looked back at the screen wall, and sure enough, there it was! He wanted to kick and scream, but he was so

worried about Bogey, he pushed it out of his mind. 'Just grab all the papers, so we can show my mum and dad later,' he whispered.

The friends stuffed everything up their jumpers. Then it was back to the search for Bogey. The men were clearly out to kill him, which meant that Bogey might be . . .

That was when Frank felt a tickle in his nozzle.

'This way,' he said firmly.

CHAPTER 51

'POP ITS CLOGS!'

'**O**pen the bag, I want to see,' said Willamina haughtily as she walked towards it, dodging cobwebby old toolboxes lying around the disused garage at the front of ICU HQ.

Billy bent over to rip the top of the plastic body bag, his luxuriant tash hanging down either side of his mouth like mini pigtails.

Willamina gasped.

Not at the face tails. At the dimply green domed head that appeared.

Billy tried not to look in case he retched.

'Urgh!' Willamina cried. It was much fouler than she remembered, with a flaky mouth and closed eyes bordered by pointy, translucent eyelashes that looked like sticky stalagmites. Its cheeks were plump now too. Not like when she'd hosed one of them into a hollow. Goodness knows what this horror was and how those Pickerty-Boops had bred it! All artists - especially the penniless ones - were just so dangerous. **'ENOUGH!'** she shouted. **'POP ITS CLOGS!'**

Billy and Steve rushed to an old toolbox in the corner and grabbed an axe.

'QUICK, QUICK, CHOP, CHOP!' chimed in Willamina.

The brothers lifted their weapons.

'After three,' said Billy, looking down and (suppressing a retch) watching the thing's face momentarily morph into a pound sign.

'One ...'

'Two ...'

'Thr—'

CHAPTER 52

REEEEETCH!

'**G**ET AWAY FROM HIM!'

Frank and Tiffany burst through the door.

'No you don't.' In a split second, Billy had grabbed both children by their arms – HARD.

'Oh, we never get to "three",' said Steve grumpily, lowering his axe.

'How did you get here?' cried Billy with menace. Every second the thing stayed alive was another second they weren't getting their money.

Frank and Tiffany wriggled to get away, but Billy's grip

was too tight.

'The brats. I should have guessed,' said Willamina, striding towards them, her eyes now glowering. She turned to the Bashers accusingly. 'Didn't you realize you were being followed?'

Billy went to say something, but Willamina held up her hand, then pointed to two chairs by the door. 'Just tie them up there. Now you're here, children, you can watch it die.'

Frank and Tiffany kicked and scratched. But Billy and Steve were too strong and within seconds, the friends were bound to the chairs with plastic cable.

'We know you planted the rats and are trying to steal our home,' Frank shouted. 'But leave our friend out of this.'

'Oh, but your friend's very much a part of this!' Willamina replied nastily. She didn't care if the brats had found her out. Snozzle was as good as hers now anyway. She blew her still-runny nose. 'How dare you breed it in MY castle and have it trespass in MY garden!' she spat. 'And how dare you snoop through my things! Bashers, KILL IT!'

'After three ... AGAIN,' said Billy, grabbing his axe and

whirling it through his fingers like a menacing baton.

'ONE ...'

Frank closed his eyes. He couldn't bear to look. All hope of saving Bogey was evaporating into an antiboog (which - if you don't know - is the nothingness in your nostril where a bogey used to be).

'TWO ...'

'But you can't kill him!' Frank blurted in desperation. 'He's a miracle of life!'

'A miracle of life?' scoffed Willamina. 'It looks like a pile of bogeys.'

'That's because he is!'

'THR— What'd you say?' came a gruff voice.

Frank waited for a *chop* sound, but it didn't come, so slowly, carefully he dared to open his eyes.

The men's arms were frozen mid-air!

'I said he's made of bogeys!' he repeated, stunned at the effect his words were having. 'Mostly mine,' he continued, 'but some of Tiffany's now too. You see, I built a bogey tower, and it came alive when lightning struck it in that strange storm the other night.'

'**Wha—?**' cried Billy. '**B-BOGEYS. GLUP!**' His axe clattered to the ground, as he retched – **REEEETCH!**

And then he couldn't stop.

REEEEETCH! REEEEETCH!

Sorry, nose-pickers, but it did go on for a very long time.

And then ... **POP!**

An explosion of thoughts connected in Willamina's head too: the brats wiping snot on the pavement, the thing's gloopy green body, its bobbly pustules, its gooey webbed feet. It couldn't be. And yet – she poked its forehead. A slab of sticky snot stuck to her palm. *Tasse de thé de bogeys*

de saucisse!

'GET IIIIITTTT!' Willamina screamed at the Bashers, utterly repulsed. **'WHAT ARE YOU WAITING F—?'**

But she never got to the end, 'cause with a sudden rustle of plastic, Bogey burst out of the body bag and leapt high into the air crying, **'GOO-GOO-GOOEY!'**

HE WAS AWAKE!

CHAPTER 53

AGILE GREEN MONKEY

I n a flurry of snot and ooze, Bogey's gelatinous body sailed through the air like an agile green monkey to grab a dangly light fitting – **'GOOOOOOOO!'** – which he used to swing towards (you guessed it) Willamina's beehive!

Then the next parts happened so quickly, nose-pickers, they all blurred into one.

Ready?

ONE.

See them?

No? OK. I'll break them down:

Number 1) 'NO!' cried Willamina, shielding her head, but - **BOING! SQUELCH!** - Bogey landed on it anyway, before bouncing back into the air and out through the door to the warehouse, blowing a big loud raspberry.

'**FOLLOW THAT MONSTER!**' screamed Willamina, wiping glop from her hair.

But the brothers wouldn't budge. Because - well, Billy couldn't, he was too busy retching. But there was something else too.

You see, in Bogey, Billy had met his **WORST NIGHTMARE**: a living breathing **BOGEY**. And it made his skin crawl and his head whirl and his arms jitter and his eyes pop and his tongue flop and his toes tingle and his chest tighten and his

heart flutter and his stomach knot and his bum – you get the picture. And for the first time in his life – **REEEETCH!** – he wanted something MORE than he wanted MONEY. He wanted **OUT**. No. He **NEEDED** out.

'What's our m-motto, Steve?' he mustered mid-gag.

'Don't scrub your armpits with the loo brush?'

'NO! **REEETCH!** It's "Wheeler-dealers always win!" But only if we're alive and I'm gonna die if we carry on. Ma'am? **REEEETCH.** You can keep your money!'

'*YOU CHEMISE DE NUIT, YOU BROSSE À DENTS!*' Willamina cursed, but Billy's mind (and stomach) was set.

And now she had a number two to deal with.

Sorry, did I say 'a' number two? (Nose-pickers, no one had done a number two. Somebody might have needed one, but nobody had done one.) I meant 'Number 2'. As in:

Number 2) The slugs suddenly catapulted themselves off Tiffany's head, and quickly oozed enough slime over the plastic cable for Frank and Tiffany to slip their hands free. **SCHLOOOP!** And … they … were … free!

'WHA—?' Willamina exclaimed.

Then it was –

Number 3) A quick scoop-up of the slugs by Tiffany, and a dash through the door.

Frank followed, grabbing a chair on his way out to wedge under the garage door handle and prevent the enemy from following them.

Once outside, the friends dashed to Tiffany's bike – Frank on the pedals, Tiffany on the seat, Bogey in the basket – and rode like the wind back to Snozzle Castle.

Mum, who was carrying the burnt broccoli quiche she'd made for dinner, heard them burst through the front door.

'You're back! Did you enjoy your bike ride?' she said, rushing into the hall.

Then she stopped dead, dropped the quiche and screamed!

'AHHHHHHHHHHHHH!'

CHAPTER 54

BETTER START PACKING

'**W**hat a wonderful high F, my darling!' said Dad, rushing in to compliment Mum, then stopping to scream himself. You see, neither parent had ever seen a real-life bogey monster before, so they had a bad case of the heebie-jeebies.

'Everyone, meet Bogey!' was all Frank could muster over the cries, which went **ON** and **ON** and **ON!**

Bogey and Tiffany huddled together by the front door, covering their ears.

Then Frank had had enough.

'STOP!' he yelled.

And to his surprise, they did.

'W-what's that?' said Mum, pointing.

'He's my friend, Bogey. I told you about him earlier, but you didn't believe me.'

Mum looked incredulous. 'The bogey tower that got struck by lightning and came alive?'

'Yes, but that's nothing compared to what's going on.' Frank took a deep breath. He had to tell them everything. And he had to make them believe him. 'Willamina Honk's really Willamina CONK,' he said firmly, 'the descendant of Dad's biggest fan. She's been here in disguise and knows about Bogey, and the cameras and the rats are all her doing, and she's going to be here any minute to kill him and reclaim the castle.'

There was a heavy silence.

'Pull the other one,' said Dad. 'Which friend have you dressed in that costume? It looks like something I'd use in a film. I bet if I look for a zip . . .' He lifted one of Bogey's arms, but . . . 'Oh!' A string of snot yo-yoed from his fingers.

'**GOO-GOO-GOOOO!**' gurgled Bogey, which meant, 'How rude!'

Dad looked queasy as he gazed at his sticky hand.

Bogey scooped his armpit goo back with a roll of his eyes.

'Did you hear what I said?' cried Frank. 'There's a bad person coming to get Bogey and steal our home!' Frank was surprised by how forceful he sounded. 'Look.' He handed his parents the contract and other papers he'd crumpled up his jumper. They looked at them with expressions of horror.

Then Tiffany pulled out the plans of Snozzle Castle and talked about the ICU HQ's wall of screens and all the cameras in the house. Everyone looked up and, sure enough, there was a camera just above the front door.

Next, Frank spoke about the sling-snot and guano in the East Wing. He didn't care who knew about his bogey-picking habit now or whether he got in trouble for it. He just wanted to save Bogey and his home. He even felt relieved when it was all finally out in the open.

Then Tiffany explained about how the slugs had helped them escape, parting her hair to show the hard-working slimers lying like exhausted jelly babies.

Dad took a look at the underlined part of the contract again, then rushed off, appearing seconds later with his copy.

'Mine says the same! *If the castle gets choked with verm* . . .' His voice tailed off. 'I always thought these clauses were just Henri joking around. But maybe he meant it?' He looked at Mum and Frank. 'My darlings. I never minded signing all those one-penny film contracts, but the castle? I'm so sorry. I should have been more careful.' He hung his head. 'I think we'd better start packing!'

CHAPTER 55

BIG GROUP HUG

'**W**AHOOOUUUUULLLLL.'

It wasn't Frank howling (it was Honkerty's weird hedgehog, in the bushes somewhere along Honkerty-Honk-Honk), but it was exactly what Frank felt like doing. *This can't be true!* he thought. *Willamina can't have won the house! But there it is – in black and white – on the first page. And probably on the sec—!* 'Uh? Hang on . . .'

Frank rushed over to his trembling father. 'Look! Willamina's contract is one page long; yours is two! Maybe there's something in yours she doesn't know about. Can I see?'

'Appendix,' Frank read out. (Which means extra information at the end of a document. Or – if you prefer – a document within a document at the end of that document. Got it? This one was handwritten.)

Some things are more important in life than others, Stanley. You know my beliefs about mythical creatures. Under the following true-life circumstances, you get to keep the castle no matter what, if:

★ vampires invade and you fight them

★ you become a real-life werewolf and need a place to hide

★ a rare and weird creature ever calls Snozzle its home

HC

The appendix was signed and dated at the bottom. Frank, Tiffany, Mum, Dad and the slugs (and even Lucy Longlegs, who'd broken off from singing 'Spinning You a Yarn' to watch) all turned to Bogey with wide eyes.

'**GOOLIEMALOOLIE!**' Frank cried. 'You're RARE! And WEIRD – in the best possible way, I mean! YOU'RE why we keep the castle. **YOU reverse the vermin clause!** WOW! You're the BEST thing that's ever happened to me!'

'**GOOOOOOO!**' replied Bogey, in delight.

And Frank flung his arms around his friend with a joyful smile – until he looked up and saw Mum's pale cheeks. Then that familiar ball of guilt squeezed his stomach.

'Frank, I don't know what to say,' Mum replied with a tremolo. 'This all feels so unreal.'

'A-are you going to —' Frank couldn't get the words out. 'I mean . . . you and Dad have always hated me picking my nose. I wouldn't blame you if' – he felt silly saying the next bit, but he said it anyway – 'you stopped loving me.'

'Are you kidding?!' said Dad. 'Forget the castle. Bogey's the personification of the mysteries of life! Plus, he'd look

FANTASTIC in a movie!'

'Frank Bear Horace Pickerty-Boop!' scolded Mum, finally getting a grip of herself. 'There is nothing on this earth that could stop me and your father loving you! Not even a monster made of your *SNOOOOOOOOOOT*,' she sang.

'I'm just sorry we didn't believe you before,' added Dad.

They strode over the splatted quiche towards Bogey and held out their hands. He took them. And Dad touched the undulations on top of Bogey's head. 'Ha! It even feels a bit like your curls, Frank.'

And before Frank knew it, he'd been pulled into a big group hug with Mum, Dad, Tiffany, the slugs, and the only bogey monster ever to have walked the earth.

The End

NO, WAIT!

SORRY, THAT WASN'T THE END!

Dearest nose-pickers! I wish it had been. It was a happy moment. Which is more than I can say for what's about to happen.

But please do read on.

CHAPTER 56

SAY BYE-BYES!

Suddenly, the sound of gravel crunching under heavy wheels drifted into everybody's ears, followed by Willamina Conk's nasty voice: **'BRING ME THE ABOMINATION, THEN GET OFF MY PROPERTY!'**

Frank looked through the hall window to see their neighbour hanging out of the ICU van window.

'Bogey, we've got to hide you!' he said.

'No,' said Dad, stepping in (like grown-ups so often do). 'This is our home. And Bogey's our family, now. Nobody's hiding or fighting. We're all going to talk this through like intelligent adults.'

Bogey trembled at the idea, but he'd seen enough violence for one day (which was half his life!), so he nodded and they all stepped outside.

At the same moment, Willamina got out of the van, brandishing a long hosepipe attached to the water tank and trailer she'd stolen from ICU HQ, and she was feeling all the more powerful for it. She was also *SIZZLING LIKE FIRE!*

'*I'M SIZZLING LIKE FIRE!*' she yelled.

Because she was.

She was *SIZZLING LIKE FIRE* because when she looked at that castle, she knew it - the only thing she'd ever been denied - was finally hers for the taking. She was *SIZZLING LIKE FIRE* because despite the bogey monster's escape, she'd remembered the cheek incident and now knew exactly how to kill it - without the Bashers! And she was *SIZZLING LIKE FIRE* because once a conquering Conk, always a conquering Conk!

'It's over,' she cried with a wicksmirk, holding up the

hosepipe nozzle like a gun.

'You're right about that,' said Dad, striding over the gravel towards her. 'But you're not squirting anybody today—'

'The hose!' Frank whispered to Tiffany in panic. 'She knows water kills Bogey!' He, Tiffany and Mum moved in front of Bogey to make a protective wall, just in case.

'—and you're not taking our castle, Ms **CONK**.' Dad emphasized the 'Conk' part. 'Look!' He thrust the appendix under her nose.

'I doubt that,' Willamina scoffed. But as the words **'rare'**, **'weird'** and **'keep the castle no matter what'** jumped out at her in her uncle's handwriting, she felt her entire prawn-like body fill up with anger, which turned to a hatred so strong (I'll call it **HATEY-HATEY-HATE-HATE**) that her teeth chattered and her arms jerked.

'NO!' she shrieked, the hatey-hatey-hate-hate swelling in her strangely hairy bunions. This wasn't right! **'CURSE MY ODD IDIOT OF AN UNCLE!'**

Then she turned towards the others. 'How dare that

thing stand between me and my inheritance!' she shrieked, her voice going all deep and guttural for the last part. She'd wanted it dead before, but that was nothing compared to now.

'Say BYE-BYES!'

CHAPTER 57

RUN TO THE DUNGEON

PSSSSSSSSSSSSSSSSSSSSSSSSSSSST!

It was Dad who went down first, with a big, cold squirt right in his face.

Then Willamina stepped over his sopping body and headed straight towards the others.

'Take that!' she squealed, squirting short, powerful bursts at Frank, Tiffany and Mum to break up their wall and get to Bogey.

PSSSSST! PSSSSST! PSSSSST!

'**ARGH!**' cried Mum as she slipped over in her violin

slippers.

'**NOOOO!**' screamed Tiffany as a blast whipped her head, sending the slugs hurtling towards the castle wall.

'**MEEEEP!**' went Slim (which meant 'aim for the softer rose trellis').

SPLAT!!!! (Don't worry, they were shaken, but alive.) Frank turned to shelter Bogey with his own body, but – **PSSSSST** – the jet was so strong and cold, his whole body shook. 'I can't hold it off much longer,' he shouted. And sure enough, seconds later, Willamina had squirted him to the ground.

'**BOGEY, RUN TO THE DUNGEON!!!!!**' he shouted.

And Bogey tried. But he was already waterlogged, and soon, Willamina had knocked him straight off the gravel on to the muddy lawn by the moat.

'Take that!' she squealed with a giggle as she forced Bogey backwards towards the gloopy water.

'This is for the trespassing!' **PSSSSST!**

'This is for standing in my way!' **PSSSSST!**

'This is for existing. **FULL STOP!**' **PSSSSST!**

And before Frank knew it, Bogey was teetering on the edge, with squidgepeas pearling over his entire body.

Frank tried to run towards him to help, but any time he, Tiffany, Mum or Dad got close, Willamina held them back with jets of spray.

'PREPARE TO SQUELCH YOUR LAST!' Willamina cried at Bogey. Then, turning to the family, she shrieked: 'Pickled-Poops. Enjoy the show!'

PSSSSSSSSSSSSSSSSSSSSSSSSST!

The full brunt of the jet hit Bogey in his bobbly midriff, causing him to fly off the edge of the moat and into the air: **'GOOOOOOOOOOOOOOOOOoo!'**

'NO!' Frank got there the second Bogey hit the water, but it was too late! Bogey's thick green body had sunk like a heavy stone.

BLUP-BLUP!

Two big bubbles rose to the surface, and then . . . NOTHING.

CHAPTER 58

THREE-FOOT MOUTH!

'**Good riddance. Ha!**' Willamina spat nastily, then re-adjusted her beehive.

Frank was just about to dive in to save Bogey, when . . .

A loud splashing sound filled the air, followed by the **blup-blup-blup** of a thousand rising bubbles. And from beneath them in the moat rose the biggest eel Frank had ever seen.

It was glistening brown, with a silver belly and black slippery eyes the size of car wheels. And as it twisted and turned, it rose out of the slimy water and opened its dripping, three-foot-wide mouth, and there inside it was ... **Bogey!**

The eel spat him out on to the moat-side path, then went back under with a big **PLOP**.

Everyone – Willamina included – stood rooted to the spot, goggle-eyed. Then Frank came to, and rushed to Bogey, who was lying in a splotch, skinny as a wet cat and dripping like a swamp monster. The water had washed much of his bogey body away, and he wasn't moving.

'**You're evil.**' Frank turned to Willamina and wiped water from his eyes. Or was it tears? 'You can't just kill someone over a contract.'

'**WHY NOT? I can do what I want.**'

Frank looked down at Bogey's lifeless body.

'Because everything that's alive has the right to be here. Just because you don't like someone, or they stop you from having what you want, doesn't mean you can destroy them! We don't like you either, Willamina Conk, but we're not trying to wipe you off the face of the earth, are we? All of us, whether we're made of flesh or bogeys, whether we're grey or stripy orange (Frank was thinking about the slugs), whether we walk on legs or flutter like a bat, we all have a right to be here!'

'Oooh, I've never had it put to me like that,' Willamina said haughtily, before looking thoughtful for a teeny-tiny second. Then she shook it off. '**Now, time for your friend to disappear.**' And rushing forward, she raised her hose once again!

Frank flinched. Mum flinched. Dad flinched. Tiffany

and the slugs flinched.

But then something amazing happened.

Willamina's face screwed up.

And her mouth opened. And –

'A–CHOOOOOOOOOO!'

Out came the biggest, gloopiest, stickiest glob of snot her honker had ever sneezed. And can you guess where it went, nose-pickers?

Oh yes!

Straight on to the very thing she wanted to kill: Bogey.

SPLAT!

The physical change was immediate:

What had been translucent became opaque; what had been scraggy fattened up – not a lot, but enough to fill Frank with hope, as he and Tiffany quickly added some extra glob-nuggets of their own.

'*TOUR EIFFEL*, **NOOOOOOO!**' Willamina yelled, raising her hose in retaliation. But it was too late for that, for suddenly a battle cry filled the air (not really, it was Honkerty's weird hedgehog trying out an elephant impression, but the timing was perfect), and the ground around her feet came alive with the pattering of seventy-three rats, two foxes, seven red squirrels and a badger. And the air above her head filled with the flutter of a thousand bats (led by Binky) and four barn owls.

Then cheered on by the entire Pickerty-Boop crew (Tiffany and the slugs included), the angry creatures chased Willamina Conk off the castle grounds, with a nip and a flap and a couple of well-thrown acorns (courtesy of the squirrels).

'Is Bogey OK?' cried Mum, rushing over with Dad.

'I don't know,' Frank answered, frantically replenishing his friend's scrawny body with every snot ball he could muster. 'He won't open his eyes.'

Tiffany gently dropped the slugs on to Bogey's body so they could make him some goo.

Then everyone joined in with a pick and a slop to put Bogey right.

'It's not working,' Frank blubbed. 'I think the animal thing might have finished him off.'

'Oh sweetheart, I'm sorry,' said Mum, putting her arm around him.

Tiffany stifled a sob.

But then Frank's nose began to tickle!

'**GOOLIEMALOOLIE!**' Bogey *WAS* alive!

𝕿𝖍𝖊 𝕰𝖓𝖉

(for real this time)

No, sorry.

Wrong again. PFFFFT! There's an epilogue.

What? You don't know what that is?

It's a story after the main story. And only the best books in the world have them!

EPILOGUE

As spring turned to summer and summer turned to autumn, a lot of things had changed in Frank's life. Willamina had moved out of Honkerty Village the very night she'd been chased out of Snozzle. And she was clearly a changed woman, for though no one knew where she'd gone, they often received designer lunchboxes full of bogeys all the way from France.*

---

* Why had she changed, nose-pickers? Nobody knows. Maybe Frank's speech had finally hit home? Or maybe she just wanted to keep the woodland animals at bay? Or maybe . . . Oh I don't know. But she was changed, so let's leave it at that.

And Bogey's body had been replenished multiple times over by the entire Pickerty-Boop family (especially Dad, who secretly admitted that when no one was looking, he always picked his honker).

But that's not all . . .

Remember that old portrait of a dainty-nosed king in the East Wing?

Well, it turned out to be the only portrait of William the Conkerer left in the entire world. And it was worth a pretty packet. Can you guess how much?

One million?

No!

Two million?

No!

Three point seven million?

No. Let me tell you.

Fourteen million, five hundred and seventy-nine thousand pounds and

twenty-seven pence!

Needless to say, the Pickerty-Boops flogged it faster than you can say 'renovate my mansion', and the whole of Snozzle Castle was now a building site. But not just a building site for the renovations of their family home. They were also building . . .

Here, I'll let Frank and Bogey show you.

Look, they're holding a banner that says:

You see, as Frank and Bogey had got to know each other better, Frank had discovered that his gloopy little chum - aside from being clever and brave and amazing with animals - had developed a taste for giving his family a good, friendly fright with his **GOO-GOO-GOOEYs**. Frank had started to wish he could turn Bogey's scaring talent into something that would benefit both his family and the whole of Honkerty Village.

'Why don't we turn the East Wing into a spooky attraction?' he suggested one day. 'Like a haunted house, or something? We could call it the "Snozzle Spook Site". Bogey could hide and scare people as they walk through the **SPOOOOOOOKY** rooms and corridors.' Frank emphasized the word 'spooky' for effect. 'And in the evenings, we could put on a live show with all the bats and rats, and Tiffany could get the slugs to perform their circus act.'

'Yes. And I could *siiiiiiiiiing!*' sang Mum.

'And I could show my films!' said Dad. 'You're turning into quite the entertainment entrepreneur!'

'Goo-goo-gooey!' said Bogey, creeping up behind them and making them all jump.

But their screams quickly turned to laughter.

So that was settled then, and the plans were drawn up.

And tonight was the pre-opening spectacular. The house and its **SPOOOOOOOKY** East Wing weren't finished yet, but the family had built a big stage over the moat and were about to give their future clients a taster of the shows to come.

'Are you ready?' Frank asked Tiffany. He was in charge of making sure everything ran smoothly.

'YES!!!!' she screamed excitedly, smoothing down her sequined jumpsuit. She was opening the spectacle with Sammy, Violet, Peach and Slim performing circus acrobatics. And it was just what she'd always dreamt of!

Frank peeked nervously through the curtains at the audience. It was dark, but he could make out old Mrs Sniff at the front by Tiffany's mum and dad and her great-gran, and they were all looking excited; and on the third row, there was Walter Wills with Gary Plonk, Bo Jacobs (and Squishy) and Mrs Wirrel (poodles in tow), who were looking ... well, they were looking at a giant bag of Bally-Wally Balls, deciding which one to scoff first.

Then, with a crack of thunder, the music started – an upbeat pop song by Lucy Longlegs and the Spiders' Cabaret called 'Snot Ball Disco'. There were even a few backing vocals by Honkerty's weird hedgehog. Though how the song had been recorded was a mystery to Frank. (I'm no good at technology, nose-pickers, but scan this and you should be able to hear it.)

bit.ly/snotballdisco

Frank ran onstage to much applause. 'Good evening,' he shouted, his heart all a-flutter. 'This time last year, no one would have thought this possible, and yet here we are, just weeks away from opening the Snozzle Spook Site. And so tonight, starting our **SPOOOOOOOOKY** spectacular is … **the WONDERFUL … the FANTABULOUS … SLUG AGILITY CIRCUS!'**

A drum roll sounded and cheesy fake lightning flashed through the air. Then big screens magnifying the slug action clicked on to much *oohing* and *aahing*, as Sammy, Violet, Peach and Slim began a succession of tricks that culminated in Slim somersaulting three metres through the air on to Peach's eye tentacles. The audience went wild. Tiffany was elated.

Five slug tricks later, and it was Mum's turn to entertain, with a funny opera aria she'd written for the occasion called 'A-Chooooo' (you can hear that here too).

bit.ly/a_choooo

Then Dad showed his new horror comedy, called *Swamp Monster Comes to Tea* and starring – can you guess? **Bogey**, of course. It had all been filmed in the Spook Site.

Then, for the grand finale, it was Bogey's turn to perform. Lit up from the rear behind a screen (so as not to reveal his true bogey identity – who knew if he'd be accepted?), his stubby, domed silhouette orchestrated what *The Honkerty Times* would soon call, 'The Most Mysterious Animal Show of the Century'. It was a flowing, magical spectacle of swooping bats and dancing rats, each wearing tiny costumes with lights that made their twirling and whirling look like stardust.

Standing there, listening to the crowd's relentless clapping, Frank looked at Bogey and Tiffany, and grinned.

Whoever would have thought that a bogey tower of his own making could cause such joy?

It was a happy ending indeed.

And so, dear nose-pickers, let's leave our heroes to their celebrating. And please excuse me a moment while I pick my nose. Sshhh! For yes, I admit that I, the author of this book, am a nose-picker . . . and a rather excellent one at that. I told you I wasn't, but I lied. I'm sorry. Can we still be friends?

EXTRA PICKINGS!

BOGEY ALERT!

BOGEY ALERT!

YOU ARE ABOUT TO READ A NOSE-PICKER'S GUIDE TO BOGEYS.

DO NOT SHOW THIS TO GROWN-UPS.

I REPEAT: DO NOT SHOW THIS TO GROWN-UPS.

MOST ADULTS WILL NOT BE ABLE TO STOMACH THIS GUIDE, AND WILL TRY TO CONFISCATE IT.

YOU HAVE BEEN WARNED.

A NOSE-PICKER'S GUIDE
TO BOGEYS

In addition to the definitions given on page 145 for snozzle crumpet, sneeze baby and cakey flakey, and also squidgepea on page 168 and antiboog on page 231, please find below a list of bogey types to look out for. Most are in this book. Others are just my favourites!

Right, here's the guide, in alphabetical order:

BRITTLEBERRY: *a crisp, fragile booger, shaped like a berry. Brittleberries are more common in summer, when the weather is hot, as they lack moisture. DO NOT try to roll them. As their name suggests, they are brittle, and crack under pressure.*

CHUMPCLUMP: *a small cluster of bogeys, like a tiny bunch of grapes. Lucky you! As they are already 'clumped' together, no assembly is required for adding to your own bogey tower (should you be making one).*

CLINGENGLOB: *a frustrating bogey, recognizable by its refusal to unstick itself from the wall of your nostril. If you retrieve a clingenglob, you can give yourself a pat on the nose.*

CRINGEBLOB: *a bogey you don't know is visible. A cringeblob may hang out of your nose or be stuck somewhere on your face. Either way, you don't know it's there until someone points it out.*

FRESCGOO: *a fresco of bogeys stuck on the wall, revealed only when furniture (primarily a child's bed) is displaced. When an adult discovers a frescgoo, they usually faint or scream A LOT.*

GLOB-NUGGET: *an unusually large 'nugget' of snot. Glob-nuggets can be hard or soft in texture. What makes them nuggets is not their consistency, but their shape, which is not dissimilar to that of a chicken dipper.*

GOO-WOOOOOOOOOAH: *a misleadingly long, stringy bogey whose name reflects the startled cry of its owner as it comes out. Goo-wooooooooooahs always start small, but get longer and longer the more you blow, often yo-yoing out of your nostrils. In a way not dissimilar to slug goo, they are perfect for holding bogey towers together.*

SLING-SNOT: *a specialist bogey identifiable not through colour or texture, but by the fact it is flying through the air having been launched from a slingshot. If you hear someone shout 'sling-snot', it might be best to wait for the SPLAT before looking for it . . .*

SNOZGOLD: *a small, golden-hued bogey, usually hard, like a hunk of gold. Bogeys tend to be green, so snozgolds are both rare and valuable. Just don't try to open a bank account with one. Only one bank on earth will accept them, but, alas dear nose-pickers, I can't remember where it is.*

TICKLETOOT: *a light, feathery bogey that both tickles your nose as you breathe and causes a whistling sound. Tickletoots can be fun if you are musically inclined; annoying if you are not.*

UFB (UNIDENTIFIED FLYING BOGEY): *a sneaky little greenie that whooshes out of your nostril while you're talking to somebody. If this happens to you, there is nothing you can do except watch it fly.*

LYRICS

'SNOT BALL DISCO'

By Lucy Longlegs and
the Spiders' Cabaret

Snot ball disco
Step into the light
Greenie greenie
Forget all your strife

Snot ball disco
When you pick your friends
Greenie greenie
Love never ends

When you're feeling down
  at the end of the day
Just Pick It
Just Pick It
Just Pick It
Yeah!

If you're feeling shy and can't
  think what to say
Just Pick It
Just Pick It
Just Pick It
Yeah!

Snot ball disco
Step into the light
Greenie greenie
Forget all your strife

Snot ball disco
When you pick your friends
Greenie greenie
Love never ends

There's a dance you can do when you're
with your friends

Touch your nose, poke your
   finger in the air
Then you turn around
   and clap your hands
and boogie like you just don't care
When you do the bogey boogie
The bogey wogie boogie,
The bogey wogie boogie woogie woogie
You got to stand up tall
Beneath the disco ball
And boogie wooggie wooggie wooggie
wooggie.

Say greenie - greenie
Say greenie - greenie
Say greenie greenie - greenie greenie
AAAHHHH!

When you're with your friends and can't
think of a game
Just Pick It
Just Pick It
Just Pick It
Yeah!

When you're at your school, why not
do the same
Just Pick It
Just Pick It
Just Pick It
Yeah!

Snot ball disco
Step into the light
Greenie greenie
Forget all your strife

Snot ball disco
When you pick your friends
Greenie greenie
Love never ends

'A-CHOOOOO'

By Mum

Have you ever had a tickle in your nose?
A-Chooo
It gets you from your head down to your
toes. PFFFT
Then there's nothing left to do
But let out a sneezy, snotty, sloppy, sticky
A-CHOOOOOOOOOOOOOO

Don't try to hold it in
It'll make you feel so grim
Your eyes will pop with nasal slop

If you keep it all inside
It'll come out your behind
And who wants snot around their bot?

Just let rip - go for the goo
It's the only thing to do.
Just let rip - it's a breeze
It's the only way to sneeze.

A-chooo
A-chooo
A-chooo

Don't let that tickle win.
It's better out than in.
Or your ears will ooze with nasal goos

Children round the world
All you boys and girls
Accept your goo - A-CHOOOOOOOOOO!

WILLAMINA CONK'S FRENCH INSULTS

CROQUE MONSIEUR - *Cheese and ham toastie*

FERRY POUR CALAIS - *Ferry to Calais*

HARICOT - *Bean*

SAUCISSON SEC - *Cured sausage*

PANTALON DE CUIR - *Leather trousers*

TASSE DE THÉ DE BOGEYS DE SAUCISSE - *Cup of tea of bogeys of sausage*

CHEMISE DE NUIT - *Nightdress*

BROSSE À DENTS - *toothbrush*

TOUR EIFFEL - *Eiffel Tower*

ACKNOWLEDGEMENTS

Dear publishing peeps, friends and family (insert your name here), this book is for you.

No, sorry.

It's for me.

Only me.

What?

Oh OK, then. I s'pose you can have some of the credit.

In fact, you can have all of it, because honestly, without you, *Monster Bogey* would not exist and my heart would not soar every time I pick my nose.

And so, to my agent Sam Copeland at RCW, for launching my publication journey and making my dreams come true. Thank you. I couldn't be in better (or funnier) hands.

To my editor, Rachel Leyshon at Chicken House, for your fantabulous sense of humour, goldmine of ideas and mind-bogeyling sense of structure. I'd happily slap your name on the cover next to mine.

To everybody at Chicken House – Barry Cunningham, Jasmine Bartlett Love, Rachel Hickman, Esther Waller, Fraser Crichton – for believing in me and bringing Bogey to life! It's an honour to be part of the team.

To my fantabulous illustrator Owen Lindsay, for working magic with a pen. I'm so lucky you said yes.

To SCBWI's Undiscovered Voices competition squad and my fellow UV 2020 winners, for seeing potential in my bogeys, and becoming my writing family and friends. You rule.

To Ollie Paquin, for being my official child beta reader. You will receive a signed copy if you say Bogey-Bogey-Bum-Bum five times before you next step into your classroom.

Also, a big wad of gratitude to the best musicians and composers I've ever met – Xavier Bussy, Sebastien Joly and Camille Troillard – for bringing 'Snot Ball Disco' and 'A-Chooooo' to life. I couldn't be prouder.

And finally, to my family – all of you, but especially my parents, and Pascal and Max – for inspiring me to write. I love you.

GOOLIEMALOOLIE!
THANK YOU EVERYBODY!